Deborah stood to greet Joab as he opened the gate and came in, striding over to stand in front of her.

"Oh, Joab," she said softly, "I'm so glad—"

But he interrupted her roughly. "Was my gift not good enough, that you send it back unopened?" His voice was low but angry.

Shocked and confused, Deborah protested, "Oh, no! I did open it. The robe is beautiful—far too beautiful for me to wear. Did you not get my message?"

"That you would not wear my gift? Who are you to decide what I shall purchase? It is for me to choose what I wish to give. Do you think I want you to look like a servant girl when you accompany my mother?"

Suddenly Deborah was furious, though she too kept her voice down. "Do you think then that I look like a servant girl? Do you think the clothing my father provides is not good enough?"

"Good enough for what? Certainly for a shepherd's daughter, but not for my—not in my household."

"But I am not in your household."

DEBORAH

Of Nazareth

DEBORAH
Of Nazareth

EDITH E. CUTTING

DAVID C. COOK
PUBLISHING CO.

David C. Cook Publishing Co., Elgin, Illinois 60120
David C. Cook Publishing Co., Weston, Ontario
Nova Distribution Ltd., Torquay, England

DEBORAH OF NAZARETH
©1991 by Edith E. Cutting

Designed by Richard Schroeppel
Cover illustration by Rick Johnson
First Printing, 1991
Printed in the United States of America
95 94 93 92 91 5 4 3 2 1

Cutting, Edith E.
        Deborah of Nazareth
            1. Marriage—Fiction. 2. Jesus Christ—
Fiction. I. Title.
PZ7.C9953De   1991
ISBN 1-55513-948-5   91-10898
Fic—dc20   CIP
                                                AC

*For my niece who also bears
this ancient and beloved name.*

Also by Edith E. Cutting

Elizabeth of Capernaum

1

With a satisfied little laugh, Deborah climbed down and sat on the lowest branch of the old olive tree. It was at least a year since she had climbed to the very top.

She wished Onan had been there to see how far she had gone. He was the one who had taught her and his sister, Judith, to climb when they were little. Now he could not take time to climb trees or play games. He was eighteen years old and had his own flock of sheep to watch over. Sometimes he and her father pastured their sheep near together. Her father said Onan was a good shepherd.

Today she had been too restless to sit at her loom and work on the rug she was weaving. If only she had her own home and family to spin and weave for, like her older sister, Sarah. That would be different. She wondered what Sarah was doing right now. Did she ever wish she could run or climb trees the way they used to? Or did you forget about that after you were married?

Deborah looked up again through the gray-green leaves. From high on her favorite branch, she had been able to see her father standing quietly by his sheep as they were feeding. In the other direction she had seen their house and the sheepfold on the edge of the village of Nazareth. Beyond the village, she could see the road leading off to the south. Her father took that road to Jerusalem every spring at Passover time, but her mother had been ill so long before she died that Deborah had not gone in years. She could hardly remember the Holy City. As she sat on the low branch, she dreamed of going again and seeing the temple of the Lord.

Suddenly a scornful voice startled her. "What is a young woman like you doing in a tree?"

Deborah jumped to the ground. There was her father's uncle staring angrily at her, with a younger man beside him.

"I—I didn't know anyone was near," she murmured, blushing.

"Surely your father has work for you to do at home. Did not your mother teach you to bake and to spin?"

Resentfully Deborah lifted her head. "My mother—" she said and then stopped. Surely her great-uncle knew that her mother had taught her these things before she died. Deborah glanced at the other man and then, embarrassed, looked down again. Tall, he was, with intense, dark eyes and a thick, brown beard. He was a stranger to the village, and yet she had a feeling she might have seen him before.

Quickly she made a gesture toward the sheep in the distance. "My father is there," she said. "I must return to the house." Bowing her head, she hurried by the men and down the path.

When she got to the house, she looked into the water jar. It was only half full, and her father would want fresh, cool water for supper. She stirred the bean porridge in the kettle at the edge of the fireplace and then went to the door again. The shadows were getting longer, but it was still too early to set barley cakes to baking. Instead, she picked up an empty water jar and started for the well.

Still angry at her uncle, she murmured to herself, "If he only knew how my mother taught me that year before she died!" Deborah remembered times when her mother could hardly speak for the pain. Sometimes she had just had to point or nod her head. *He only came to her funeral*, she thought. *What does he know of her really—or of me, either?*

Two other women were at the well when she got there. They were chattering to each other, and at first Deborah paid no attention. Then she heard her father's name, and she listened more closely.

"Yes, it was Elihu the older man asked for. He said

he was Elihu's uncle, but he did not say who the younger man was."

"But what did they come for? He hasn't been here since Elihu's wife died, and strangers don't usually come off the main road this side of Nazareth."

"Well, who knows," the first woman answered. Deborah noticed both of them look at her, and then they turned away. "Perhaps he's looking for a lamb," she continued. They both began to laugh.

Deborah could not see anything funny about that. Her father sold many lambs for sacrifice because he had some of the best sheep anywhere near Nazareth.

When the other women had finished drawing their water and left, Deborah filled her jar. She swung it to her head and started carefully along the path.

By the time she was back at the house, dusk was closing down. Her father would be leading the sheep into the fold and would be home soon for supper. Quickly she stirred up dough for the barley cakes and dribbled in some honey. Her father liked things sweetened a little. She patted out the flat cakes carefully and set them by the fire to bake.

They were nearly done when she heard her father's voice. "We have guests for supper tonight, Daughter," he said as he entered the door. Deborah looked up. There were her father's uncle who had scolded her—and the other man. Quickly she bowed her head. Scold or not, they were guests in her father's house, and her father must not be ashamed of her.

She brought a basin and poured water for their hands and feet, then handed them a towel while she did the same for her father. Hurrying to the jar of fresh water, she dipped a cupful for each of them. She did not look up, but she felt sure the stranger was looking at her. Carefully she dipped three bowls of porridge and set them on the cloth. She sliced cheese and fresh cucumbers and filled a bowl with olives, as her father invited the men to sit with him.

Deborah would wait and eat when they were finished. Now she slipped the hot barley cakes onto a plate. As she placed them before the men, she glanced at her father and he nodded toward the back of the room. Deborah brought the wineskin and poured a cupful for each man. Then she bowed again and stepped back to the darker part of the room. There she knelt quietly to be ready if the men needed anything further.

As she saw the stranger take another barley cake, she smiled to herself. She was glad she had put in the honey. Then her lips tightened. It was her mother who had taught her to do that. Suddenly she wished she could show them the fine threads her mother had taught her to spin. Why had her uncle criticized her in front of this other man when he had not even seen what she could do?

At last the meal was over. The men went outside. While Deborah ate her supper, she could hear other men from the village talking with her father and the stranger, but before they came back in she had laid out their sleeping pads. She cuddled down on her own and slept.

When Deborah woke the next morning, the men had already gone. She munched a few olives and a leftover piece of barley cake for breakfast, thinking what she would do that day.

She picked up the pads on which they had slept and shook them out the doorway. Then she hung each one on the sturdy bushes at the back of the yard in the sun. Neatly she cleaned the hearth and swept the floor. At last she took her spindle and wool to the shade of the acacia tree beside the front door. There she could see what was going on in the village and even visit with some of the neighbor women.

Next door, Judith, her best friend, was spinning by her doorway, too, while she watched her little boy creeping around in the sand. Azi was already eight months old. Deborah smiled as she watched him creep to his mother and pull himself up.

"Soon he will be walking," she called to Judith.

Her friend nodded proudly. "Surely he is strong like his father," she replied. "My husband says he will be a great man in Israel when he grows up." She picked up her son, but he pushed away and slid to the ground again.

Deborah sighed. When would she have a husband, and a son like Azi? She was a year older than Judith—fifteen last year in the month of Elul. Yet her father made no move to find a husband for her. And truly, what would he do if she were to be married? Who would keep his house and bake his bread and entertain his guests?

At the thought of guests, Deborah remembered the tall man who had come with her father's uncle. Almost as if Judith were reading her mind, she called, "Do tell me about your guests of last night. I hear that the older man is your father's uncle, but who was the younger one? Is your uncle a marriage broker that he comes now to see your father?"

"No, no," Deborah answered. "Nothing was said, and I know not the younger man. Perhaps he is a neighbor traveling from Jerusalem." She bent over her spinning, her face flushed at the thought of the younger man's keen eyes. But maybe?

"My father's uncle was not even pleased with me," she added. She smiled ruefully at Judith. "You remember the big olive tree we used to climb when we were children?"

As Judith nodded, Deborah went on, "I climbed it again yesterday. I was so uneasy. I wanted—I don't know what I wanted. Do you remember how Onan would lift us up to the first branch?"

Judith laughed. "Yes, I remember. You were always quicker than I. But you are too old to be climbing trees now. You should be—" She broke off without saying "married," and hurried to pick up Azi.

"Yes," Deborah answered. "That's what my father's

uncle thought." She sighed again. "But how can I be married and leave my father alone? And who will speak for a maid with a father to live with them?" She clapped her hand over her mouth, ashamed to have said that, even to Judith. Hurriedly she gathered up her wool and went into the house. It would soon be time to make a lunch and carry it to her father.

2

At noon Deborah packed bread and cheese and onions, with a flask of water, and went to find her father where he would be watching his sheep. She took her spinning also, for she loved to sit by him and work on the wool. It was different from sitting at home alone to spin.

When she got there, she found Onan with him. Everybody liked Onan. Besides, his flock was small as yet, so his sheep did not need too much grass. Shepherds with bigger flocks were often glad of his company to pass the time.

He and her father had been laughing at two lambs that were jumping and playing, when they saw Deborah coming with her basket. "Ah," called Onan, "it is already the hour of noon, and here comes the lady with a basket of good things." He swung a bag with his own lunch around on his belt as Deborah set her basket in the shade of the olive tree. Quickly he and Deborah's father looked over the flocks to make sure all was well; then they sat down to eat.

Before Deborah joined them, she went to Onan's flock. "Blackie," she called, and a lamb came running. It was the little one she had taken care of for Onan when it had been born. It had been one of twins, and its mother had preferred the other. Onan had been so busy with the sheep and new lambs he had hardly slept for three nights. Deborah had taken that lamb home and fed it along with one of her father's that was too small to stay with the flock. Now she scratched this little one's head and fed it a piece of bread before she went to her father's flock and called that one.

When she came back where the men were eating, Onan smiled at her. "How times are changed," he said, before he bit into a piece of cheese. "Here you are, providing food for your father, but only a few minutes ago, it seems, you were climbing olive trees."

Now she was no longer embarrassed at what she had done, nor even angry with her uncle. Onan always made things all right, she thought. "It really was only a few minutes ago," she said, smiling. "Just yesterday when I was going back to the house after bringing Father's lunch, I remembered climbing with you and wanted to try it again." She told him of climbing the tree the day before, and of her uncle's scolding.

Onan laughed easily. "Surely he must have been surprised to see such an olive drop from the branches.

No wonder he snapped at you, little one."

But Deborah's father was not laughing. He finished his meal quietly and went to lead his sheep a little farther away.

Soon Onan, too, went to his sheep, leaving Deborah to spin by herself in the shade. This was one of her favorite times of day and one of her favorite places. She looked out over the field where the red anemones gleamed like little flames in the sun. She remembered picking some of them to take to her mother, when she had been a little girl. Now and then she could see a hawk circling over the field.

As she dropped her spindle in her lap and leaned back against the tree trunk, she could see a sparrow flitting overhead. Then she spotted its tiny nest above her. She wondered if there were eggs in it, or if the baby birds were already hatched. Sleepily she listened to the locusts' rasping hum.

Then there was a rattle of stones and a shout. Deborah jumped to her feet and looked around. Where was her father? She saw Onan hurrying toward her father's flock. Deborah dropped her wool and ran, too, though she tried not to scare the sheep.

"Onan," she called. "Where's Father? What happened?"

By the time she had caught up with him, he stood on the edge of the old quarry where building stones had been cut for houses in Nazareth.

As she looked over, she could see a little brown

lamb on a ledge below her, but farther down lay her father. Shocked to see him so still, she whispered, "Is he—?"

"Stand back," Onan said. "I will go down. He must have tried to get the lamb, and the edge of the stones gave way. There is a better path over there. You wait here."

Then she saw her father move. He was trying to push himself up, but she could see blood on his face and along one leg.

Onan started to the left, then turned back. "Watch the sheep," he said quietly. "They know you. Speak calmly to them."

Deborah nodded, catching her breath. How could she speak calmly with her father hurt? And Onan—suppose he fell, too? She bit her lip hard and turned back to the flocks. Onan's sheep were grazing quietly farther down the valley, but two or three of her father's sheep were standing still facing her, their heads up as if they were afraid and might run.

"Bright Eyes," she called softly as she walked toward them. "Long Nose, eat the good grass." How she wished she knew all their names the way her father did. Still, if she kept her voice soft, they might think she did. "It's not time to be thirsty yet, Bright Eyes." She reached out toward the nearest one. The sheep sniffed at her hand and then went back to feeding. Deborah watched as the others dropped their heads to continue nibbling at the grass. "Bright Eyes, Long Nose, you

beautiful sheep, you are safe. Eat peacefully now."
Deborah went on talking in the same quiet tone, hardly
thinking what she said, but talking to reassure the
sheep.

She turned halfway so she could keep an eye on
them and still watch for Onan and her father. At last
she saw their heads coming up over the lower edge of
the rocks. Breathing a sigh of relief, she gave thanks to
the Lord. Her father was leaning on Onan and limping
clumsily, but he was walking. He was alive!

Deborah waited, still talking quietly to the sheep as
the men came slowly toward her. The side of her
father's face was bleeding and so was his left arm.
"Abba!" she called softly.

He shook his head. "It's not too bad," he said,
wiping some blood from his forehead. "My leg got
scraped and cut on the rocks, but it's not broken." He
was using his staff like a cane. "You did well to keep
the sheep quiet," he said. "I was foolish to lean so far
over. I thought I could reach little Brownie with my
staff, but a piece of the bank gave way and I slid."

Onan looked down the valley at his sheep. Two
were straying from the rest. "I'll have to to call them
back," he said to Deborah. "You stay with your father
till I come again. Then I'll go down a different way to
get little Brownie."

Deborah moved closer and took her father's arm,
as she heard the lamb bleat again.

"No," he said, moving away. "I'll lead the sheep to

water. Deborah can stay and talk to the lamb while you get your sheep gathered and started for home."

Deborah was looking at her father. He was very pale, and the cuts on his head and leg were still bleeding a little. She glanced at Onan and saw him motion toward her father.

"Deborah will go with you," Onan said firmly. "I will lead my sheep to join you. They will follow your sheep if I get them started. Then I will come back for Brownie."

Deborah saw her father's face tighten, ready to protest. She knew what he was thinking. A shepherd all these years, and now to leave one of his lambs!

"Come, Father," she said gently. "Lean on me, but you must call your sheep. I kept them still, but I know they would not all follow me."

He hesitated, then straightened his shoulders. Turning to Onan he said, "If you will rescue my little Brownie, you shall add her to your flock."

Onan started to protest, but Deborah shook her head as her father put his arm around her shoulders and started along the path.

"I will meet you at the three oak trees together," Onan said, and hurried on toward his flock.

It was nearly two hours later when Deborah and her father got to the house. The sheep took forever to drink, and her father had had to stop to rest several times himself. Then he made sure they were settled in the fold for the night before he would go on to the house.

By that time his face was gray with tiredness and pain. Deborah helped him to a stool and had just poured water into a basin to wash off the drying blood when her Aunt Anna came bustling in.

"What happened? What happened? Here, let me wash the wounds. You get your father a cup of wine. What happened? Did the wolf attack him?"

3

"WOLF!" EXCLAIMED Deborah, turning to stare at her aunt. "There's no wolf this near the village." She hurried to get the wineskin and pour a cupful. "My father fell. The sharp rocks cut him so."

"Now food," commanded her aunt. "I knew these were not tooth marks, but they could be scratches. And there is a wolf. It's been seen twice near the flocks. My brother barely saved a lamb from it."

By this time Deborah had uncovered the coals and put unleavened bread to bake. From the cupboard she took cheese and olives and onions.

"Tsk, tsk," her aunt whispered as she washed the long cut down the leg. "Wine again, Deborah," she called. "Pour gently to cleanse the cuts. Now bring oil to keep the skin soft. Your father will be stiff and sore in the morning."

"And not the first time," said her father, looking

more like himself. "I thank you, Anna, my good wife's sister, for your care. Now go to your home in peace and with my blessings."

"And mine, too," said Deborah softly as she walked toward the door with Anna.

Her father had just taken a bite of onion with his bread when Onan came to the door. "Did you get the lamb?" asked Deborah's father.

Onan nodded. "Yes, he was cold and hungry but not hurt. I've settled him in the house for tonight." He smiled. "In the morning, he will be ready to frisk around again."

Deborah saw her father look sternly at Onan. "With your flock," he said.

Onan protested, but her father could not be moved. "Do you think I want a lamb I cannot take care of? I would be reminded every day. Besides, I owe deep gratitude to you. What is one little lamb?"

Anna had turned back from the door when Onan came in. Now she asked, "Did you hear about the wolf? Have you folded your sheep securely?"

Onan frowned and glanced at Deborah, but he answered courteously. "I have heard, but my father says there has been no wolf near for several years. He thinks perhaps it was a fox that scared someone's sheep."

"A fox!" she exclaimed. "My brother certainly knows a fox from a wolf!"

Deborah could see her aunt was ready for an evening's argument, so she quickly broke in. "Perhaps tomorrow someone will see it again. Thank you, Aunt Anna, and good night to you!"

As she turned back into the room, her father smiled at her. "More and more like your mother," he said. "She always knew how to turn away Anna's chatter. It's early yet, but get some bread for Onan and we will finish our supper quietly."

"No, no," Onan objected. "My mother will be looking for me. I just came to tell you I will take your sheep with mine tomorrow. You will need to be quiet," he added, glancing at the long cut, "but your lead sheep knows my voice, and the others will follow her."

"We shall see," the older man answered. "You are very kind, but we shall see."

That evening Deborah's father seemed very still. Finally he said to her, "Come sit by me, Daughter."

"Is your leg aching?" she asked. "Or have I done something to be scolded for?" she teased, sitting down on the floor by him.

"Not you," he answered with a smile. He put out his hand and stroked her hair the way he used to do when she was a little girl. "Not you," he said again. "It is I who have been selfish. With your mother gone, I have kept you here and you have eased the loneliness, but you should have a home of your own."

"Oh, no," she protested, not wanting him to feel hurt. "I have been happy here. Where else should I go? Or with whom?" She shut her mind to the face that flashed across it.

"That is what I have been thinking about," he answered. "My uncle came to ask my plans and to suggest a husband for you, but I did not say yes or no. Have you thought of a husband who would please you, my daughter?"

Deborah bowed her head. "It is for you to say," she murmured.

Her father went on. "I had thought of Onan. He is young, but he is a good worker, and he has always looked on you with favor."

Deborah's heart jumped. Onan. Of course. He was always kind, and if she were married to him, she could still live here in the village. She would be near her father and Judith and other people she knew.

But her father was speaking again. "Now my uncle has proposed another man. Joab, the son of my uncle's cousin, is the overseer of his father's many shepherds. He lives in Bethany, but you saw him when they stopped here two days ago."

Deborah gasped. The tall, brown-bearded man. He must be much older than Onan. And he had seen her climbing a tree. No wonder her uncle had been angry. She blushed and put her hands to her face.

Her father did not seem to notice. He was staring into the dark at the back of the room. His voice went on softly, thoughtfully. "He has money and position. He will be a wealthy man when his father dies. You will have a fine home. My uncle says he is a good man, a leader in business, and his family could choose a wife of higher rank. But he had seen you with a black lamb one day when he was passing on his rounds."

"Oh!" Deborah remembered now. No wonder he had looked familiar. She thought of that day. She had been trying to get the lamb's mother to nurse it, but without success. Finally the sheep had turned and butt Deborah, making her lose her balance. She had tumbled and slid down a bank to the road, holding the lamb in her arms. Unhurt, she had gotten up, laughing, and shaken herself to smooth down her dress. As she set the lamb down on its shaky legs, a man had been passing by. He had not spoken, of course, but as she had glanced up she had thought his eyes were laughing at her. Quickly she had picked up the lamb and climbed back up the rocks. Was that the man? It must have been. She caught her breath. To be her husband? She began to smile as she thought again of the handsome stranger.

Her father was waiting for her to speak. But now she thought of her uncle's angry face. "Our uncle was not pleased with me," she said finally. "Twice I have appeared foolish. No doubt the man's family would not be pleased with me either. They may have withdrawn their offer."

"No." Her father shook his head. "My uncle talked with me after you had served supper and before we lay down to sleep. The family offers a generous bride price."

Remembering the supper, Deborah was suddenly angry. A man who wanted a wife because she could make sweet barley cakes? Was he a glutton then, that she would be married to? And was he to be her husband instead of Onan because he had much money?

Her father had seen the change in her face. "What is it, my daughter?" he asked gently. "Without your mother to advise, you must tell me. I want to do what is best for you."

Deborah bowed her head as she whispered, "I know you do." She was ashamed. Just that morning she had thought to blame her father because she was not married like Judith. She had not realized all he must consider. She had thought he could easily arrange a marriage if he only would. Now he was asking her to decide, and she could not.

Onan or Joab? Both good men. Onan had been a friend for years, but his family was no richer than her father. They could probably not offer much of a bride price to help her father when she went to a new home. Joab would be wealthy, her father said. Perhaps he could offer enough money to pay someone to keep house for her father, or buy more sheep, but—

Her father's voice was quiet as he said, "Let us go to our beds. Think on what I have said, and we will talk again before I send an answer."

Deborah did not sleep well that night. She knew her father was not sleeping, for she heard him sigh as he turned on his mat, trying to get comfortable. Twice she brought him a cup of water, and he drank thirstily. The second time she wiped his forehead and hands with a damp cloth, and he finally went to sleep.

Before dawn Onan came quietly to the door. "Is he sleeping?" he whispered.

"Now he is," Deborah answered, "but he did not sleep well all night. Can you manage the sheep?"

Onan nodded. "His sheep and mine are used to being near. I will lead mine first, and his will follow. I will come back tonight after they are folded, to see how he gets on."

He turned away, and Deborah went back to her father. He was still sleeping, but he must have heard her move. Quickly he sat up, then groaned as he moved.

"Stay quiet, Father," Deborah said softly. "I will wash the sores with warm water and put on olive oil to soften them."

"There is no time for that," he protested. "The sheep will be waiting."

"Onan is leading them with his," she answered. "You know he will take good care of them. He knows most of them by name, and he has already gone to the fold."

Quickly she came with a basin and cloth. She sponged the cuts on his face, his arm and leg. She had just finished when her Aunt Anna came to the door.

"Up already?" Anna asked. "How are the cuts?" She came closer and touched them gently. "A little feverish," she said, "but not bad. I brought some ointment to use on them today. If you stay quiet, they will soon be better."

"Father is so strong, he will heal fast," Deborah answered proudly as she accepted the little jar of salve.

"They are better already," her father said, struggling to his feet. Deborah hurried to him, and he grasped her shoulder to steady himself. His mouth was tight, but at last he raised his head and smiled ruefully. "I guess the shepherd needs a shepherd," he admitted. Looking down at the ugly scab on his leg, he shook his head. "If a sheep had scraped herself like that, I would have carried her home."

Deborah laughed, relieved. "Shall I carry you to the fold then?" she asked.

He patted her shoulder as the pain eased. "I will walk a little now, and then come in for breakfast." He paused and again his mouth tightened. "I never thought I would leave my sheep for a day, but Onan is a good boy. He will lead them well." He raised his head with determination. "Tomorrow I will be ready to go with them again."

Anna looked at him. "You always were a stubborn man," she said. Then turning to Deborah, she added, "Use the salve today, and by evening he will move more easily."

4

THAT EVENING ONAN CAME to the house again to see how Deborah's father was progressing. "I am as good as any old ram that got in a fight," her father assured him with a mile. "Tomorrow I shall be with my flock again."

Onan smiled back. "Do you not trust me with them? I'll admit they were a little restless today without you, but they settled down and grazed—after a while."

"I trust you indeed," Deborah's father replied warmly, "but tomorrow I shall be with my sheep."

Onan nodded. "They will be glad," he said simply.

The next morning her father was up and moving around when she awoke. "Rest quiet," he said. "I will take bread and olives so you need not come this noon."

"No, indeed," said Deborah, jumping up. "Let me put the salve on your leg before you go, and I will bring the midday meal. I will make new bread," she promised, smiling at him. "Eat a piece of yesterday's and some olives before you go." She brought the ointment jar and knelt beside him.

When she had finished spreading salve along the healing scabs, she sat back on her heels and watched him hurry to the door. He limped a little, but she knew he would not be content till he had gone to his sheep and spoken to each one of them.

By mid-morning Deborah was happily making new bread. While it baked, she brought fresh cucumbers from the garden and packed them with a piece of cheese and a small cake of figs. This was a special thanksgiving lunch. She smiled to herself as she started up the hill. She was as anxious to get to her father and make sure he was all right as he had been to get to his sheep.

When she came in sight of the flocks, all was peaceful. Onan's flock was farther up the hill, but her father's sheep were feeding quietly as he stood watching them. When Deborah came in sight, he looked up and smiled. "My favorite lamb," he said as she approached.

She smiled back at him. "My favorite shepherd," she replied, looking around for a shady place to lay out the food.

"The oak tree near Onan's flock is a good place," her father suggested.

Deborah was about to protest his walking farther,

but she realized in time that that would only hurt his pride. "Your sheep must have been glad to see you," she said instead.

He nodded. "I have spoken to each one by name, and they are quiet," he said. "I will walk with you."

Before Deborah could lay out the lunch, Onan joined them under the tree. The three sat companionably in the shade, saying little but watching the sheep.

Not lingering over his lunch, though, her father soon limped back to his flock. She saw him move along the outskirts of the flock, touching every sheep and lamb separately, as if he were saying a blessing on each one. Though Onan's sheep were nearer, he, too, soon stood and walked slowly toward them. They were closer to the thorny bushes, and he needed to make sure none got its wool caught in them.

Deborah took up her spinning, and with her hands busy, looked out over the valley. The almond trees toward Nazareth were almost past their time of blossoming, though there were still a few pink or white puffs of bloom. She leaned back and looked up at the vivid blue sky. The scattered clouds were like sheep themselves. In her heart she gave thanks to God that her father had not been more seriously hurt, and that they could enjoy this day together.

Suddenly she realized that several of Onan's sheep nearest her had stopped eating and were standing still, facing a tangle of briars. She stood up quietly so as not to startle them with a quick movement and tried to see what had disturbed them. She could see Onan walking carefully toward them, calling first one and then another by name.

Then she saw a slight movement in the bushes. The mother of the little black lamb stamped her foot, but the branches moved again, and Deborah caught a glimpse of an animal's ear. It couldn't be—a wolf so near the village? It gave a sudden leap toward the littlest lamb, and in the same instant Deborah screamed.

She ran toward the wolf with her spindle raised, and the sheep scattered, but before she could reach the lamb there was a thud. The wolf whirled and disappeared. Her father was hurrying now with his staff in his hand, but Onan was already there, another stone ready in his slingshot.

Deborah was shaking. "Was it a wolf?" she whispered. "Could it be?"

"A wolf indeed," her father answered.

"Right in daylight!" exclaimed Onan.

"Perhaps an old one," added her father, "lost from his pack and desperate. We must watch closely lest he come back."

Onan was already calling his flock together, but even as they came toward him he pushed into the bushes where the wolf had disappeared. Deborah's father stood quietly looking over his own flock that stood fearfully, heads up and ready to run, but he talked softly to Onan's sheep to reassure them. Then Onan's voice came from among the thorn trees. "No need to worry," he called. "The stone has done its work."

He came out of the bushes. "I will bring a spade this evening and bury it." With a glance at Deborah's face, he took her cold hand in his. "Come," he said. "There is no need to fear." Softly he, too, began talking to his sheep. "See, even little Blackie is not hurt."

Deborah nodded. Kneeling, she cuddled the lamb into her arms till her own shaking stopped. Then as she stood up, the lamb jumped and ran to the rest of the flock.

Deborah picked up her spindle and looked ruefully at the tangled yarn. By this time Onan was making the circuit of his flock to be sure all were calm. As he came back by her, he called gently, "It will soon be time to take the sheep to water. Are you all right?"

She nodded as she held up her tangled wool. "But look at my yarn. My uncle would surely say I do not know how to spin."

Onan laughed. "But how many girls know how to fight a wolf with a spindle?"

The next morning was the beginning of sheep-shearing season. Deborah knew that her father, with other shepherds in the village, had made arrangements to have some of the skilled shearers stop there before going on to the bigger flocks near Mount Carmel. Like other women in the village, she was up early to start baking the dozens of loaves of wheat and barley bread that would be needed, and set meat to roasting.

Before it was quite noon, the village women had set out piles of bread and of cheese, with bowls of olives and onions and leeks. There were dried figs and dates for the men's sweet tooth, and cold water from the well to quench their thirst. Soon the men began gathering, hungry and thirsty from their morning's work. Many of the same men had been here before. Deborah saw Onan and her father going from man to man to thank each for his work and to ask about his family or neighbors in other villages.

They did not speak to Deborah or the other women, but once when her father glanced at her, she saw his nod of pride. Onan was saying little as he walked among his elders, but Deborah felt good as she watched him. *Someday,* she thought, *Onan will be one of the elders of the village, and younger men will look up to him.*

The men had finished their main meal, though a few were still munching on dates. They were beginning to visit again when a silence fell over the group.

Deborah looked around to see what had happened. There stood the overseer who had come with her uncle before. He was saying nothing, but the men were quickly standing up and starting back to the flocks. Deborah looked for her father, but he had gone back to his flock while the shearers were still eating. Where was Onan? Gone, too. She looked at the other women. Surely the married women should offer this man food, but they were busy and pretending not to see him.

Suddenly Deborah realized they were waiting for her to serve the man who had been her father's guest. Bowing her head, she picked up a platter of bread and approached him. Silently she gestured for him to sit down, and without lifting her eyes, she set other dishes before him and hurried to get a cup of water.

"Many thanks," he said softly. Deborah was so startled by a strange man's speaking to her that she glanced up and for a moment met his eyes. Dark and intense, as she remembered them, but something more. Smiling? Not quite. Admiring? Deborah blushed and turned away quickly.

5

WHEN JOAB HAD FINISHED his meal and gone on, Deborah and the other women ate and then cleared away the remains of the food. "He is really handsome," Judith teased, "and anyone can see he thinks you are, too,"

Deborah shook her head, but before she could think of anything to say, another woman added, "Yes, truly, your father will be proud of such a son-in-law. Your uncle knew what he was doing. You can see he could not stay away."

"No, no," Deborah protested. "He only came to oversee the shearers. That is his business."

"Yes, and a good business it is. Will you even speak to us when you have a fine house in Bethany?"

Deborah shook her head helplessly. "You do not understand. He stopped only for food." She frowned thoughtfully. "But why did the men hurry away?" she asked, thinking of her father's way with workers. "Why did he not speak with them?"

"Ah, well," said one of the older women as she nibbled on a last date. "He does not carry a whip as overseers used to do in Egypt, but the whip is in his eyes. Why else does he hold such a position if he cannot command?" She shrugged and turned away, muttering, "You will learn."

Deborah shivered. But Judith came up behind her. "Don't pay any attention," she whispered. "She's just jealous. Her husband doesn't amount to a cup of watered wine. Surely this man looks kindly on you."

A few days later a message came from Deborah's sister, Sarah. She lived in Bethany, near Jerusalem, but Deborah had never been there. Her mother had been ill so long that they had not gone to the festivals since before Sarah had been married. She had now sent word by her husband's brother Korah, a merchant returning to Nazareth. Could Deborah come take care of her little Elon till her new baby was born? Could her father spare Deborah for a month or more? And Sarah's husband, Lamech, wanted someone older to be with her when her time came. Could Aunt Anna come to be with her?

When Deborah heard the news, her face lit up. "Oh, I haven't seen Sarah in almost three years. Elon will be a real little boy instead of a baby. He won't know me!"

Then she sobered. "But how will you be?" she

asked her father, as they sat together in the courtyard. "I can't go and leave you here alone. I could bake some bread to leave, but not for a whole month. It would get stale."

Her father smiled. "You are a good girl, Deborah. I am fortunate to have such daughters. But Onan was way ahead of you. He was there when Korah stopped with the message, and he asked me to stay with his family till you returned."

"Oh, you have it all planned!" Deborah exclaimed. "But how can we go? I can walk, I'm sure, but Aunt Anna— She will go, won't she?"

"Even there we are blessed. Korah goes often to Jerusalem with loads of wool, and he said he could spare a donkey for her to ride."

"When will he go? When should I be ready? I need to wash the clothes and scrub the shelves to leave all neat and—"

Her father laughed. "The Lord makes time for all things. It will be four days or maybe five before Korah has his business finished and travels south again."

Deborah whirled around and started dancing the hora by herself around her father, stepping to one side and then the other. Suddenly she realized they were not alone, but the tips of someone's fingers were touching hers, and his feet were following her pattern. Onan? Happily she looked up, but instead saw Joab smiling down at her as he circled in the dance.

"Oh," she cried, clapping her hand to her mouth.

"I—I didn't see—you want my father—I will go—"

She turned hurriedly toward the house. "But wait," he said softly. She stopped but kept her face turned away. "I would not spoil the dance." He turned to her father. "Surely some happy news has come?"

Her father nodded. "Bring wine, my daughter," he said. "Our guest will sit here by me for a few moments."

"Cold water, please, instead of wine," said Joab, and her father nodded.

Deborah hurried into the house. Her fingers still tingled from the touch of his hand. Shakily she straightened her dress and smoothed her hair. Slowly she took deep breaths to quiet the beating of her heart. Then taking two cups, she filled them with water from the big jar and went back out into the evening light.

Her father had just finished telling Joab of the plan for Deborah to go to Bethany.

"How fortunate that I, too, will be returning soon. Your daughter shall ride my donkey, and I shall accompany the caravan."

Her father protested out of courtesy, but Deborah could see that he was pleased. Joab would not hear of opposition. Before her father could say much, Joab stood up. "We will call it settled then. I will talk with Korah and set a day. I thank you for the water." He handed the cup to Deborah, then turned and left.

Deborah dropped down on the ground beside her father, her arms around her knees. She wished her mother were there for her to talk to.

At last her father spoke. "Do you not wish to journey in his company?"

"Oh, yes," Deborah burst out. "He is—he is—" She buried her face in her arms. In a muffled voice she went on, "It is very kind of him." she hesitated. "But should I? It is not meet—we are not betrothed—"

"Do you wish to be?" asked her father quietly.

Deborah sat silent. At last she shook her head. "Not yet. I am not sure. He—I never felt this way before. But perhaps I should not go with him—perhaps he thinks—"

Her father touched her hair gently as he had the other night when they had talked. "He is a good man. He will not serve you ill. And your Aunt Anna will be there, besides. You will not be alone."

Deborah raised her head and looked into the distance as her father went on, "Now let us go in and sleep. A courtesy had been shown and accepted, but it is only that. You need not fear. I'm sure he understands."

Deborah took a deep breath. She was not so sure as her father seemed, but anyway, it was for him to decide. Perhaps men thought differently about such things.

The next day Deborah did not linger when she took her father's midday meal. She hurried along the shortest path to get where he was with the flock and waited anxiously for him to finish. There was so much she wanted to do before she left.

He ate slowly as usual, savoring each bite. "You

make good bread," he said. "It tastes like your mother's used to." He sat gazing at the hills as he chewed the last piece.

Deborah was ashamed of her impatience. He would be lonely indeed while she was gone. She let her hands relax and leaned back against the trunk of the tree.

At last he wiped his mouth and sighed. "You should not take the time to bring my lunch," he said. "I know you have many things to do before you go. Perhaps tomorrow you can just wrap some bread and olives in a cloth, and I will take them in the morning."

"No, no," she objected, suddenly realizing how much this time with her father meant to her, too. What if he fell again while she was gone? "No, I love to watch the sheep, and it will be so long before I can sit here with you again. Tomorrow I shall bring my spindle and wool. Perhaps you can sit a little longer and tell me a story as you used to do?"

"What story would you like?" he asked, smiling at her.

She thought for a moment, then she smiled, too. "The story of David taking food to his brothers. When Mother sent me with your lunch, I used to pretend I was David."

The second day, as she had promised, Deborah brought her wool and spindle. She and her father had finished their meal, and she sat spinning as he told her again the story of the boy David.

When he had finished, they sat silent for a few minutes, each wondering when they would sit this way again. At last her father stood up. "I must go back to the flock now," he said quietly. "Sit here if you will, or go back to the house." He smiled at her. "I know you are anxious to leave all shining." He looked around. "Onan is coming along the path," he added. He raised his hand in greeting, then turned to his flock as Onan came up the hill.

"So, you are going to Bethany to visit your sister," he greeted her.

Deborah smiled and nodded. "Isn't it exciting?" she asked, her eyes shining. "I haven't seen her since she was here when Elon was born." Onan sat down beside her. "And I've never been to her home. I can hardly wait. Maybe I can stay long enough to go to Jerusalem with her and see the temple." She sat imagining it, her hands clasped tightly in her lap.

When Onan said nothing, she looked at him in surprise. "Onan, you look so serious. Aren't you glad for me?"

At that he smiled. "Of course," he said, "but I shall miss you. Here, I brought a little sheep I carved from olive wood. I thought you would like to take it to Elon." He laid it in her hands.

"Why, Onan!" she exclaimed. "He will love it." She held it up and softly traced the outline with her fingers. "I will tell him that you made it."

Onan laughed. "He doesn't know me. He was only

in swaddling clothes when your sister took him home from here."

"But I shall tell him about you. I shall tell him it looks like one of your sheep." She smiled. "If he doesn't like it, I'll keep it for myself, for I do know you and your sheep." She glanced at him and down at the toy again. "But I know he will treasure it. What little boy would not? Did you have a toy like this when you were little?"

Onan didn't answer. Deborah looked up at him and surprised a look she had not seen before on his face. She realized he had not been listening, so she hurriedly asked again, "Did you have a toy sheep when you were little?"

Quietly he answered, "I still have it. My uncle made it for me, and I used it as a pattern for this." He stood up. "Deborah," he said, then stopped.

"Yes?" she asked, standing, too.

But he shook his head and suddenly smiled at her. "Come back safely," was all he said, as he turned and started back toward his flock.

6

It was only three days after all before the wool caravan was ready. Deborah had washed her clothes and her father's and dried them in the sun. She had aired the beds. She had swept the floor and made sure each dish was washed and dried and in its proper place. In all this time there was no special word from Joab, but he was always in her thoughts.

Judith had told her how the village women were talking. They thought Joab was so good looking. But Deborah worried about other things. Would he approve of her housekeeping? Would she meet his family in Bethany? Would his mother think her good enough to be her daughter-in-law? Deborah blushed turning her thoughts to something else, but soon she was dreaming again. He was handsome. And it had been thoughtful of him to lend his donkey. Surely . . .

The days had rushed by, but now she was ready,

with her bundle of extra clothes, wool to spin for Sarah while she was there, Onan's olive wood toy, and a special plate that had been their mother's to take as a gift to Sarah. Her father was sending a skin of Nazareth's best wine to Sarah's husband.

Just at sunrise the loaded donkeys came down the street and Deborah hurried out. "Poor little donkey," she said, laughing as she held all her bundles. "He'll wish he had a load of wool instead of me."

But Joab's donkey was a bigger one than the others, and a lighter gray. It looked taller and stronger than the one behind it that her Aunt Anna was already riding.

"Oh, he is beautiful," Deborah said, petting his nose, "but surely I should have a smaller one. I'll trade places with Aunt Anna—"

"No!" Joab interrupted. "This donkey is for my— for you!" Deborah looked up in surprise. He sounded almost angry. What had she said wrong?

Her father standing beside her spoke quickly. "You are very kind. I'm sure my daughter appreciates your choice."

Deborah bowed her head in embarrassment. Of course. She had seemed to criticize his plans, when she had only meant—"I'm sorry," she whispered. "I am honored."

"Say nothing more," Joab responded in his warm, kindly voice. "For you I will always choose only the best." He helped her onto the donkey's back and stood looking up at her. For a moment she met his eyes and then hurriedly looked down as she arranged her skirts.

A little breathless, she spoke formally, "You are very kind." He laughed softly and moved on to speak to Korah.

Deborah heard Joab say, ". . . through Samaria." She was surprised, for her father had always told her it was dangerous to go that way. Korah protested, but Joab cut him short saying only, "It's safe enough. We'll go that way." And with that, the caravan began to move.

It was a beautiful morning. Excited to be starting the long trip to Bethany, Deborah looked around at the familiar countryside. The slim, dark cypress trees pointed to the sky. Here and there an ancient olive tree spread its gray-green branches. Among the stones on the hillside she could see daisies and red poppies. As long as she could see the smoky blue Galilean hills, she did not feel far from home. She was sorry they were not going to cross the Jordan River. She remembered how much fun it had been to wade across at the ford when she was a little girl.

Almost before she realized, it was noon. They had come to a well where the men could draw water, and the donkeys in the line were all stopping.

Before she could slide down, Joab was there. "The oak trees will give us shade to rest," he said, as he held his hand up to her. Confidently she laid her hand in his and jumped down. For a moment she thought that her knees would not hold her up. "Stand still," he said.

"You have not ridden so far before, but your legs will strengthen in a minute."

Deborah nodded. They felt steadier already. She slid her hand from his and looked back for Aunt Anna.

"I'll see to the donkeys now," he said. "There are olives and bread in this bundle," he went on, handing it to her. "You can get water at the well. Your aunt will join you, and I will eat with the men."

Deborah smiled up at him. "You're like my father," she said. "You think of everything."

A frown wrinkled his forehead, then quickly smoothed out. "I'm not like your father," he contradicted. "I intend to be more than a shepherd—good man as he is, of course," he added hastily. "But yes, for you, I try to think of everything. Now go." He turned abruptly and hurried away.

That afternoon they were into the hills of Samaria. The road was narrower in places, and the donkeys plodded along in single file. Deborah felt shut in and uneasy. No wide fields here for grain or grazing sheep, and the pine trees seemed darker and closer. She thought of the wolf Onan had killed and wondered if there were others here, or jackals, perhaps. She shivered and looked around, but Joab was nowhere in sight. Firmly she shrugged off her worries. Of course he was busy somewhere with the caravan. He could not stay by her.

Still, the morning's joyous sunshine was gone. Clouds were gathering dully over the tops of the trees.

She had packed a heavy cloak in case of rain, but it was in one of her bundles. She wished she had planned better. How could she get it without stopping her donkey and blocking the caravan? She hoped it would not rain before they stopped for the night. Maybe after supper Joab would come to their campfire.

She hugged herself as she thought of him. Wait till Sarah saw him! He was so tall and straight. All the other men obeyed him, and the women in the village would envy her. She tried not to think of the way he had spoken of her father.

It was nearly sunset when he came back along the line. "You're not too tired?" he asked. "There is a good place to stop for the night just beyond the narrow path ahead. I think we can get there before dark."

"Oh, no, I'm too excited to be tired," Deborah answered, smiling. She looked back over her shoulder and called, "How are you, Aunt Anna?"

"Well enough," she replied, "but I don't like this way. We should have gone across the Jordan the way we always have."

Deborah was embarrassed as she turned back to Joab and saw his mouth tighten. "My aunt is tired," she said hurriedly. "She doesn't mean to criticize."

His face relaxed as he answered, "We won't stop here anyway. There is no place for the donkeys to graze, and it is a favorite spot for robbers."

He had hardly finished speaking when they heard a rush and clatter of hoofs and shouts up ahead. "Stay here!" Joab commanded as he started to run toward the front of the line.

The pack donkeys ahead had stopped, and some were blocking the way as they tried to turn around. The drivers were shouting at them and using their prods to try to hurry them on. Deborah could see three other men mounted on light gray donkeys as big as hers. They were shouting, too, and waving whips as they tried to drive the loaded donkeys off the road and into the trees. Deborah stared, shocked and fearful. What would happen to Joab?

7

THEN DEBORAH HEARD JOAB shouting above the other voices. She could not tell the words, but she saw him gesture toward the rear of the caravan. He kept yelling angrily and waving his arms, striking one of the robber's donkeys and pointing back toward Deborah.

Suddenly the attackers stopped. The leader pointed too, then turned his mount. The others followed, and in seconds they were out of sight among the trees.

It had all happened so fast that Deborah could hardly take it in. She realized she had been holding her breath and clutching the donkey's mane. Now she began to laugh shakily. What an adventure! And everybody was all right because Joab was so brave. He had run at the brigands without even a club in his hand!

Now he was helping Korah and the other men straighten out the line and get the donkeys going again. It was nearly dark, but soon they would be through the narrow pass. Then they could make fires for supper, and probably Joab or Korah would set guards so they could rest safely. Deborah could hardly wait to talk it over with Aunt Anna.

When they finally stopped, Deborah was still so excited she could hardly eat. "Wasn't Joab brave?" she chattered to Aunt Anna. "He certainly scared off the bandits. Do you suppose he even had a dagger? They must have had them."

Aunt Anna shrugged. "What is one dagger against three men?" she asked. "I said we should not have come this way. If they had only listened to me—"

"Well, he didn't need a dagger, anyway," Deborah answered. Then she laughed. "One of the women at shearing time said he had a whip in his eyes. I didn't know what she meant then, but whatever it was, he knew how to use it on those robbers."

"Yes, didn't he?" Aunt Anna agreed. "But I've got one in my tongue if he ever turns his on us."

"Oh, he would never do that," protested Deborah. "He's been so kind."

They went on eating their bread and olives till Deborah burst out again,"But weren't you proud of him? I was scared, but Joab said we would be all right. He's had to travel so much. He's probably had to deal with bandits before."

"It may well be," answered Aunt Anna, as she spread out the saddle blanket. "It may well be."

Deborah stopped trying to visit. Probably Aunt Anna had been more scared than she admitted. She finished her supper and wrapped up the rest of the bread neatly. She wondered if Joab would come to their fire when all was settled. Maybe he would tell her what really happened.

He did indeed come to their fire, but so late Deborah had almost given up expecting him. "Still awake?" he asked softly as he dropped down beside her. "You're not afraid, are you?"

Deborah shook her head. "Not with you here," she whispered. Then she looked up at him, and his dark eyes held her own. "Oh, Joab, I was afraid when you were driving off the raiders. You were all alone without even a staff. I thought they might have daggers. But you were so brave you even scared them. They must have thought you had weapons or more men coming. What did you shout at them that made them run off?"

"Wouldn't you like to know?" he teased.

Then the smile left his face, and he struck his fist on his knee. "I told them if my—if you had been hurt—"

Deborah reached out and touched his hand. "But I wasn't, thanks to you."

He snatched his hand away and Deborah drew back, embarrassed. "No thanks to them," he was saying. "They know—" He stopped abruptly.

Deborah looked at him, puzzled. "What do they know?" she asked. "Do they know when caravans are coming through?"

He smiled. "Think no more about it, my little bird," he said. "I know my way here, and I can take care of my own. They will not bother us again."

He stood up. "Sleep now, for we will make an early start in the morning."

He strode off into the dark, but Deborah did not sleep for some time.

It was nearly dark the third day when they reached Bethany. Korah took most of the caravan on to his place of business, but Joab continued with Deborah and Anna. Deborah was afraid her sister would have given up their coming that night, but when the donkeys turned the last corner, she could see Sarah and Lamech sitting in their courtyard. Before the donkeys had reached the gate, Lamech had hurried to open it, and Sarah was beside him by the time the donkeys stopped.

Deborah jumped down and ran to hug her sister. "Oh, Sarah," she cried, "it's been so long!"

"But you're finally here," Sarah answered, kissing her on both cheeks. "I was hoping you would come today."

"And Aunt Anna, too," Deborah said, turning to her. Lamech was already helping the older woman down, and he and Sarah greeted her warmly.

Then Deborah turned to Joab to introduce him. "Joab bar Zabad," she said formally, "this is my sister's husband, Lamech bar Abed."

The two men greeted each other, and Deborah went on, "And my sister, Sarah. Oh, Sarah," she added, "Joab has been so kind. He came all the way with us and even protected us through Samaria. Wait till you hear!"

But Joab interrupted. "It has been my pleasure." He was already lifting down the bundles they had brought. "And now I know you are tired but have much to talk about." He smiled and bowed to Sarah and Lamech, and Anna. "I will take the animals away and let you rest." Quickly he slipped the donkeys' lead ropes over his arm. As he turned away, he spoke in a low voice to Deborah. "I am sure my mother will send greetings to you. But now, good night. Rest well." His smile was like a promise, and she nodded happily.

As he left, the family all went on into the house. "Is Elon already asleep?" Deborah asked. "I can hardly wait to see him."

Her sister smiled. "You can see him right now. He's so sound asleep you will not waken him."

Lamech brought the lighted lamp, and Deborah knelt beside the little boy's bed. Anna came and looked over her shoulder. "He's not a baby anymore," Deborah said softly, almost in disappointment. "Of course, I knew he would not be, but that's the way I remember him, and I longed to cuddle him."

Sarah laughed. "Well, it won't be long before you can cuddle his brother or sister." She opened a cupboard door. "Did you have supper on the way? I have bread and olives and figs in plenty."

"That will be fine," answered Aunt Anna. "I want a drink of fresh water more than anything else."

The next morning Lamech had already left to open his shop when Deborah woke up. Aunt Anna and Sarah were talking quietly, and Elon was munching on a piece of bread. Deborah sat up quickly. "Oh, I'm lazy. Why did you let me sleep so long?"

She slipped into her robe and smiled at Elon. His mother gave him a little push as she said, "This is your Aunt Deborah. Will you give her the kiss of welcome?"

Elon nodded soberly and held up his face to be kissed. Deborah knelt down and kissed him on each cheek, but then he stepped back. "Aunt Deborah?" he asked tentatively.

Deborah nodded. "I've come a long way to see you, and I bring greetings from your grandfather. Someday you will come to visit him and see his sheep."

Elon's face brightened. "Sheep?" he repeated.

"Oh, I just remembered," said Deborah, looking around for her bundles. "Onan sent you a sheep to play with." She opened one of the bundles while Elon came closer to watch. "Onan is a good friend," she explained, as she brought out the little carved toy. "Here is the sheep he made for you." She held it out, and Elon took it eagerly.

Turning it over and over, he examined the little sheep happily. "Sheep has ears," he said. Deborah nodded, watching him. "And tail," he added. He set the toy on the floor. "It stands up," he announced.

For a minute he stood, just looking at it. Then he knelt down. "I'll help sheep walk," he said, lifting and setting it down gently as he moved it towards the door.

"Say thank you to Aunt Deborah," his mother reminded him.

He nodded. "Thank you," he said, but his eyes were on the sheep as he carefully walked it out into the courtyard.

"He's growing up," his mother said. "But give him a little time to get acquainted, and he will love you more than the sheep."

Deborah laughed. "That will be a compliment indeed. But how he has grown. Tell me all about him."

There was so much to talk about: Elon, the coming baby, the trip from Nazareth, their father, Lamech's copper shop on Jericho Street. And Joab!

"He is such a fine-looking man," said Sarah. "And his family—Lamech knows of them. His father owns much land. Tell me how he came to know of you."

Deborah blushed as she remembered, but before she could answer, Elon came running in. This time he went directly to Deborah. "Tell me a story about the sheep," he demanded. "What does a sheep say?"

By afternoon he had appropriated Deborah as his own special attendant. She had to tell him over and over about the sheep and about Onan who had carved it, and about Elon's grandfather, who had many sheep.

By nighttime she was ready to go to bed almost as soon as Elon. She could hear the voices of the others as they visited in the courtyard, and was almost asleep when she heard Joab's name. She sat up quickly.

8

Aunt Anna was talking. ". . . some kind of arrangement with the brigands. I heard him shout, 'You know my donkey.' But then I couldn't hear anything more."

Deborah gasped, but then she heard Lamech's voice. "It's possible. The donkey could have been his signal. Was it different from the others? Some men consider it saves money to pay off the robber bands ahead of time and get their caravans through safely."

"Well, Deborah thinks he is wonderful, anyway, but . . ." Aunt Anna's voice trailed off.

Deborah lay back down, her heart pounding. Could it be true? Joab doing business with robbers? She remembered his saying, "They know—" But why hadn't he told her instead of letting her go on about how brave he was? She felt herself flushing in embarrassment as she turned over and tried to go to sleep.

Maybe it wasn't true. Aunt Anna didn't really know, nor Lamech either. Besides, men didn't usually talk over their business with women. Was that so terrible? He probably didn't want to worry her. He had said he would take care of her, anyway. She was smiling as she drifted off into sleep.

Nearly a week passed, with Aunt Anna watching Sarah and helping with the housework, while Deborah kept Elon busy. She took him to the village well when she went for water and sat with him in the courtyard while she spun. They went to Lamech's shop and watched him hammering copper into a big, oval tray.

Sometimes in the afternoon they walked outside the village to a field where Elon could climb on the rocks and play. Always he took his toy sheep with him. When he wanted to pick flowers, he would trust it to Deborah, but when they walked home, he carried the sheep and she would carry the flowers.

One day they were finishing lunch when Sarah gasped and put her hand quickly to her side. Deborah saw her look at Aunt Anna, but before they had time to say anything, Deborah suggested, "Let's give Elon a treat today and let him take his nap outdoors."

Elon clapped his hands. "Sleep with my sheep," he crowed.

"There's a big rock in the field where he can sleep in the shade," Deborah added.

"You take a nap, too?" asked Elon.

"Maybe," she agreed. "Anyway, I'll take my spindle

and we can stay all afternoon."

"Take some raisins for him when he wakes up," Sarah said, and added in a whisper, "Oh, hurry."

The afternoon in the field was quiet. While Elon had his nap, Deborah worked on her spinning and thought about Sarah: Was she all right? Had the baby been born yet? Would it be a boy or a girl?

When Elon woke and nestled against her, she told him a story until he was ready to play, then let him climb onto the low rocks and jump off. It was near sundown when they finally came back, Elon carrying his sheep, and Deborah a bunch of red poppies.

Deborah heard a squeaky little cry as they opened the gate. She glanced at Elon and said quickly, "Sit here in the shade and keep your sheep cool while I get us a drink of water."

As Deborah entered the house, there was Aunt Anna triumphantly holding up the new baby. "A fine new son you have," she was saying .

Sarah looked exhausted, but she was smiling as Deborah bent to kiss her and offer congratulations. "A boy! Another boy!"

Her sister nodded happily. "Send word to Lamech. He will be glad."

Aunt Anna was already bathing the baby, and Deborah watched while she gently rubbed him with salt to strengthen his skin. Then as she began wrapping him in swaddling clothes, she said, "Tell Elon to come see his new brother."

Hastily Deborah picked up a cup and dipped water to take to Elon as she told him the news.

When Lamech came hurrying home, Elon ran to meet him at the gate. "We've got a new brother," he shouted. "He just came."

"Isn't that fine!" his father answered. "You and I will have lots to teach him, won't we?"

Elon nodded importantly. "But he's asleep now. We can't talk to him till he wakes up."

One morning a few days later, a servant of Joab appeared at the gate of the courtyard where Sarah was sitting with the baby. The man was carefully carrying a bundle wrapped in clean cloth, and asked for Deborah. When she came into the courtyard, he put it into her hands and delivered his message.

"My master, Joab, sends you this robe to wear to the temple in Jerusalem. His mother goes three days from now and wishes you to accompany her."

"Oh, thank you. I should be happy to, but my sister is not yet allowed to travel. I will wait to go with her and her husband when they go to the temple."

"No reason you can't go both times," said Aunt Anna, coming out of the house. "Go when you get the chance, I always say."

"Yes," Sarah urged in a low voice. "Go now. It is Joab who asks, and you should honor his request." Deborah still hesitated, but Sarah went on, "You will be with his mother. You can get to know her—and she wants to meet you, I am sure."

Deborah's face brightened. "Yes, of course." She turned again to the servant. "Thank your master for the gift. And tell his mother I shall be happy to attend her."

He bowed and left. Deborah took the bundle inside and opened it carefully as Sarah and Aunt Anna stood by. From the folds of the covering cloth flowed a beautiful, turquoise robe.

"Oh, no," she gasped, as Sarah breathed, "How beautiful!" and reached to smooth the shimmering silk.

"But it is too beautiful, too costly," Deborah objected, hardly touching it. "I cannot accept such a gift."

"Well, I must say it is a handsome gift," said Aunt Anna, feeling the silk between her fingers. "Good quality, too."

"His family is wealthy, Deborah," her sister argued. "It means no more to him than linen does to us."

"I know," Deborah said, frowning, "but my family is not wealthy. We have never worn silk. Even your husband—and he cares much for you—he does not dress you like—like one of Solomon's peacocks!"

Sarah laughed. "How I would love to have him do so!" she exclaimed.

Deborah didn't even smile but sat looking rebelliously at the robe while Aunt Anna picked up the argument. "If it were up to me, I'd tell your father to settle things right away. He should get a good bride price if your husband can afford to dress you in silk."

"Aunt Anna!" exclaimed Deborah, blushing. "He's not—"

"Well," Aunt Anna interrupted, "you won't have a better chance." She settled herself at the small mill-stones where she had been grinding meal.

Deborah folded the robe carefully back into its covering as she spoke quietly to Sarah. "But the neighbors—what would your friends think of me?"

"They would think you are lucky," Sarah insisted. "Besides, it is a gift. You cannot insult him by rejecting his gift."

"I mean no insult. Had it been a simple gift, I would have accepted it happily, but this will call attention to me. People will know his mother and think I belong to that family."

"Well, you soon will," urged Sarah.

Deborah looked up at her slowly. "It may be." She paused, then went on. "And if that time comes, I shall do as my husband wishes. But for now—I am not even betrothed. If he thinks kindly of me, he will not wish to embarrass me." She tied the outer covering carefully. "I shall take it back and explain."

"Oh, no, Deborah!" Her shoulders stiffened as Sarah pleaded, "At least wait till tomorrow. You may think differently then."

Deborah shook her head. "No, I won't think differently."

"Then if you must, send it back by a messenger. It is not fitting that you go alone to his house."

At that, Deborah nodded. "Yes, I see. Then let us call one from the village now. Perhaps Lamech can spare a helper from the shop. Elon and I can walk there and ask. I would not run the risk of having the gown soiled. It is too beautiful."

That was agreed, but when the messenger returned, he said Joab's mother was not at home. He had left the bundle and the message.

Deborah was disturbed all afternoon. Would Joab's mother be angry? Not want her to go to the temple after all? Would she be ashamed to be seen with Deborah in her plain robe? It was good linen and well made, she thought, smoothing out the skirt of the one she was wearing. Would Joab himself be angry?

She tried to keep busy so as not to think about it. After Elon got up from his nap, she played with him in the courtyard. He used Onan's sheep to act out the stories she told him: how she had tumbled down the bank with the little black lamb in her arms, and how Onan had killed the wolf with his slingshot. When it was time for supper, he made a sheepfold of twigs and fenced his little sheep in for the night.

After the others had gone to bed, Deborah still sat in the courtyard. It was cool, and she liked to watch the stars coming out, then gradually fading as the moon rose. The night seemed peaceful after the upsetting day.

She wished she could have explained to Joab. Just sending the message seemed so cold. Her father had said he was a good man. Surely he would have understood. Perhaps tomorrow. . . .

She was just about to go to bed when she heard footsteps coming along the street. Could it be Joab? Who else would be coming at this time? She began to smile. He had realized how she felt and was coming to tell her! They could talk quietly here with no one else listening. She stood to greet him as he opened the gate and came in, striding over to stand in front of her.

"Oh, Joab," she said softly, "I'm so glad—"

But he interrupted her roughly. "Was my gift not good enough, that you send it back unopened?" His voice was low but angry.

Shocked and confused, Deborah protested, "Oh, no! I did open it. The robe is beautiful—far too beautiful for me to wear. Did you not get my message?"

"That you would not wear my gift? Who are you to decide what I shall purchase? It is for me to choose what I wish to give. Do you think I want you to look like a servant girl when you accompany my mother?"

Suddenly Deborah was furious, though she, too, kept her voice down, hoping Sarah would not hear. "Do you think then that I look like a servant girl? Do you think the clothing my father provides is not good enough?"

"Good enough for what? Certainly for a shepherd's daughter, but not for my—not in my household."

"But I am not in your household."

"You will be my guest when you ride with my

mother in the litter to Jerusalem. Would you shame her?"

Deborah caught her breath. "I had not thought of doing so. I would wish to do all honor to your mother."

"Ah, then," she could hear his voice relax, "you will wear the robe, and others as I provide." Now there was warmth instead of anger in his voice. "You are beautiful when you are proud and angry. But you must never be angry with me, only proud." He stepped nearer and took her hand. "My little one, do you not realize I can give you far beyond what you have ever had? I shall make you proud of me and all the things I can give you."

Deborah stood silent, confused. She had not meant that she would wear the robe. Surely there were other ways of honoring his mother. But he had talked so quickly she did not know how to go back to that without sounding stubborn and childish.

At last he said, "I should not be here, and it is time for you to go in. I will send the robe in the morning, with jewelry to match. Wear it with pride. Not everyone can give you a robe from Persia!"

He turned abruptly and started toward the gate. As he did so, Deborah heard his foot crunch down on Elon's sheepfold.

"Oh, Joab," she cried, "you did not step on Elon's toy sheep, did you?" Quickly she knelt to feel among the sticks. She recognized the carved shape of the sheep, but as she held it up in the moonlight, she could see one leg was broken off.

Joab laughed. "That little splinter of wood? Don't worry. I'll send him a better one tomorrow." He went through the gate and down the street, leaving Deborah on her knees.

Before she realized it, tears were running down her cheeks as she clutched the sheep and felt carefully around till she found the broken piece. "I'm so sorry, Onan," she whispered, and the whisper turned into a sob. She choked it down, but the tears kept running. She wanted her father. She wanted Onan. She wanted to be home.

At last she scrubbed away the tears and took a deep breath. Quietly she went in and got ready for bed, still holding the little carved sheep. Tomorrow she would mend it for Elon. She would tell him the wolf tried to catch it, but it got away. Smiling shakily, she went to sleep.

9

It was just getting light the next morning when she wakened to feel Elon patting her face. "Aunt Deborah," he whispered, "Aunt Deborah, my sheep is gone. The sheepfold is all broken and my sheep is gone."

"I know, Elon," she answered, "but I've got him safe." Quickly she sat up. "See?" She opened her hand and Elon reached eagerly for the little toy sheep.

"His leg is broken!" he said.

"Yes, but I can fix it," she comforted him. "Give it to me and then bring me my yarn. I have the leg right here by my bed."

Carefully she fitted the jagged edges together. When Elon brought the yarn, she wound it around and around the body and the leg till they were secure.

"Now he's got wool like a real sheep," said Elon. "Why don't you wind it all over him, Aunt Deborah?"

"What a good idea!" she agreed. She pulled a longer strand of wool. "Around his other legs, around his middle, around his tail. There, how's that?"

"That's good!" said Elon as she fastened the wool and handed the sheep back to him. Gently he took it and ran to show his mother. "See? Now I've got a real woolly sheep, and his broken leg is all better."

"Good," his mother answered, and Lamech swung him up onto his shoulder.

"Be careful of my sheep," warned Elon.

"You be careful of him," his father answered with a laugh. "It looks to me as if a giant stepped on your sheepfold. Next time build it back in a corner where it's safe. Now let's have breakfast."

"My sheep is hungry," agreed Elon as his father set him down again. Happily they all gathered around the tray while Sarah picked up the baby and nursed him.

It was well before noon when Joab's servant brought the robe again, with the message that his mistress would be ready to start the next morning. She would come in the litter for Deborah at sunrise so as to be in Jerusalem before the heat of the day.

Unhappily Deborah accepted the package. "Thank your mistress for me," she said. "I shall be ready." Slowly she turned away and took the bundle inside.

It was much later in the day when another messenger appeared at the gate. Deborah and Aunt Anna had been busy all morning, but now in the late afternoon, they were spinning in the courtyard. Elon was playing around their feet, and Sarah was resting in the shade while the baby slept.

"I bring something for the small boy, Elon," the messenger said.

"Oh, how nice," said Sarah, standing and pushing Elon forward. "What is it? Who sent it?"

Deborah said nothing, bending quietly over her wool. Sarah took Elon's hand and walked toward the messenger.

Without answering her questions, he suggested, "Perhaps the boy should sit down so it will not break when he unwraps it."

Elon sat down with his legs spread, and the man set the big package on the ground in front of him. Sarah knelt and untied the binding. Then Elon pulled the wrapping back. There stood a beautiful, big, pottery sheep. Elon stared at it.

"A sheep!" exclaimed Sarah. "How lovely! Who sent it?" she asked again, looking up at the messenger.

"My master, Joab," he answered.

"Elon, say thank you to the nice man. Isn't it a beautiful sheep?"

Elon nodded. Then he reached out and touched it. "It isn't woolly like mine," he said at last.

"But this is yours," insisted his mother. "Now you will have two sheep. Tell the man to say thank you to his master for such a beautiful one."

"Thank you," said Elon. "Did you make it?"

The servant smiled and shook his head. "My master

bought it for you in the pottery maker's shop. I will tell him you said thank you."

Elon nodded. Then he asked, "Would you like to see my sheep?" He ran over to the bench where he had left it beside Deborah, and brought it back in his hand. "See?" he said. "He's all woolly like a real sheep."

"He is a fine one," the man agreed. "Now you have two in your flock. Soon you will be a real shepherd."

Elon looked doubtful, but at last he nodded. "I'll put that one under the bench by Aunt Deborah where nobody can step on it and break it."

"That's a good idea," agreed the servant. Then he turned to Sarah. "I will tell my master you were pleased." Hesitantly, he looked at Deborah. "Do you have any message?" he asked.

Deborah had been thinking rapidly. She knew she must not shame Joab in front of his servant, but such an expensive piece of pottery. . . . It was not a toy. Really! She drew a quick breath, then said carefully, "Tell your master it was very kind of him to spend time and money for my nephew. The sheep is beautifully made, the finest I have seen."

The servant relaxed and bowed, then turned to take his leave.

The next morning Deborah was up long before sunrise. She ate only a small piece of bread and a few olives, and she had trouble choking them down. Still she must not disgrace herself by being hungry and faint as the day grew hotter.

Her hair was smoothly combed and fastened, and the robe hung gracefully about her as she waited by the door. Matching gold and turquoise jewels hung from her ears. "You look beautiful!" exclaimed Sarah. "Joab's mother will certainly be proud of you."

Deborah's mouth tightened, but she said nothing. Then as they heard the shuffle of the litter bearers' feet, she turned and hugged Sarah. "Wish me well," she whispered, then quickly pulled away. With her head high, she walked toward the gate.

Never having ridden in a litter before, Deborah wondered how it would feel. It looked like a big, open box with two seats and curtains that could be let down on each side. Six men were carrying it slung by leather straps from their shoulders. They had set it down as Deborah approached so that she would be able to step in. Now she looked quickly at the lady inside, Joab's mother, sitting quietly and smiling at her.

After proper greetings, Deborah was seated facing Joab's mother, and they started on their way. Deborah waited quietly for the older woman to speak, but she said nothing till they were well outside of Bethany. Then she turned to Deborah and said softly. "I hope you are not angry with my son."

Surprised, Deborah did not know how to answer. While she searched for something to say, Joab's mother went on. "It is hard to change one's ways, isn't it?" She reached out and touched Deborah's robe. "I hated silk when I was first married. It seemed so—slippery. But

Joab's father thought it beautiful, and I learned to like it because he did."

Deborah stiffened, and the older woman drew back her hand, sighing a little. "Joab is much like his father," she said. "He thinks that giving things is what matters. He cannot show his feelings otherwise. He is a good man, really. He gives much to the synagogue, and he sends generous alms to the poor."

Before Deborah could stop herself, she burst out, "And am I the poor, that he must give me alms for clothing?" Then as she saw the distress on his mother's face, she bit her tongue. "Oh, I am sorry. I did not mean to hurt you."

His mother smiled. "You only touched the hurt that has long been there. I had hoped that you could understand him, that you could accept with a joy that would—soften the shell he wears around himself. But I have said too much too soon. Let us forget all else. You and I shall enjoy this day."

They did enjoy it. As the sun rose higher, they watched the sheep feeding in the distance, the little lizards on the rocks beside the road, the bright oleander blossoms along a hidden watercourse, a child playing donkey with his younger brother on his shoulders.

Joab's mother talked about her childhood in a village farther south near the Salt Sea, and she asked about Deborah's home. Deborah talked of her mother and of her death as she had not been able to before, of keeping house for her father, and of her spinning.

"How I loved to spin!" The older woman sighed. "It seemed as if I had creation in my hands." She stopped, then apologized. "I did not mean sacrilege, and I have never said this except to my husband when he said spinning was not suitable for his wife. He said I should only supervise the household. But it seemed when I spun as if the mass of wool was unformed as the Torah says the earth was at first, and then I made something of it. Ah, well," she broke off, "certainly we make different things in our lives, and we cannot always choose."

She smiled at the girl beside her. "How serious we are getting. Surely to make a happy household and children for the future—these are good things, too."

Deborah sat silent. How she wished Joab would talk with her like this. It reminded her of sitting with her father and Onan at lunchtime. But Joab just told her what to do and was angry if she said anything. She could not remember her mother and father being angry at each other. Without thinking, she asked, "Were you ever angry with Joab's father?"

His mother laughed quietly. "Yes, many times. But I admired him, and I grew to love him. I wanted him to be happy with me. And the old saying is true, you know: 'A soft answer turneth away wrath.' I learned to turn away my own anger as well as his. He is a good man, and he has been good to me.

"Oh, look," she cried. "We have come in sight of the towers of the temple!"

From there on, Deborah could think of nothing but the Holy City. She watched the mighty temple rise higher as they came closer, gleaming white marble with its golden crown. Surely this was God's house, a fitting place to bring sacrifices to the one true God. There could be no other like it.

Before they were inside the walls, they began to hear shouts and cries. "Is something wrong?" Deborah asked anxiously.

10

Joab's mother shook her head happily. "No, no, nothing is wrong. It is only that life itself is noisy here. Isn't it exciting?"

Deborah smiled back at the older woman, her eyes shining, as they entered the gateway in the massive wall. She felt like bouncing in her seat the way little Elon did when he was excited. "Oh, I wish I had an eye on each side of my head like a hare," she said, laughing. "Then I could see both sides at once."

There were donkeys loaded so high that all she could see were their heads and feet. And then a line of ungainly camels. How haughty they looked! She had seen them going along the road past Nazareth, but never this close. They were so tall!

There were men in black robes, with long, black beards, and men with shaven faces. There were women in black, their hair well covered by black scarves, and others dressed in brilliant golds and greens. Deborah thought, after all, she would not be too conspicuous in the turquoise robe. Some people walked, some rode on donkeys, and a few like Deborah and Joab's mother peeped excitedly around the lowered curtains of their litters. Everybody was hurrying, or trying to. They darted into an open space and then were blocked by sheep being driven to the market or carts piled high with bundles and bales.

Slowly they progressed, getting higher and higher toward the temple. At last the litter stopped, and Joab's mother told the men when to return for them.

Awed, Deborah walked behind the older woman. She felt dwarfed by the high walls. How had men ever lifted such huge blocks of stone into place? Two or three would be as high as her father's whole house.

Everyone seemed to be crowding through the gates. "This is the Court of the Gentiles," Joab's mother explained. "Anybody can come in here. Wait a minute. I must change some money for the offering when we go inside." She stopped by a temple official and handed him a gold coin. He looked at it carefully, then at her and at Deborah. Slowly he began to count out the official coins.

While he was counting, Deborah looked at the tall colonnades surrounding the court and at the intricately carved golden vine along one wall. Then her eyes were caught by the crowds, and she watched the people, fascinated. There were women no older than she, with babies in their arms, and old women, bent and leaning on canes. Two women in brilliant robes walked by, their heads high. Deborah almost giggled—they looked as haughty as the camels had—but she covered her mouth in time. An elderly man with long, blue fringes on his robe stalked by, and then a younger one with a chip of wood behind his ear. A carpenter? Deborah wondered if her father would have worn strands of wool to show he was a shepherd.

"Come now." Deborah was startled by Joab's mother's voice. She had almost forgotten her, but as she turned to follow, the older woman began chatting again. "How different people's faces are! I could watch them forever. But we must go on into the Court of the Women. There is need for much wood for the sacrificial fires. Trees from Judea or Samaria must be cut and brought here. It is very expensive. My husband asked me to come make the offering because he cannot be away from his business."

Carefully Deborah walked along, trying not to bump into anyone as they worked their way toward the Women's Court. She wanted to see all the gorgeous carving along the walls but yet not lag behind. She must remember it all to tell Onan. Suddenly she almost stumbled, held back by someone's foot planted solidly on the hem of her gown! She tried to pull away but could not get loose. Then as the crowd moved again and released it, she saw on the shimmering silk the soiled outline of the sandal. Oh, what would Joab think? The very first time she had worn it!

She looked for his mother and saw her ahead. Deborah hurriedly pushed her way through the crowd to catch up. As she did so, she brushed against a workman with a heavy coil of rope over his shoulder. It was coarse and rough, and the fibers pulled threads in her sleeve. By the time she had reached Joab's mother, she was almost ready to cry. When they pushed through the big doorway into the Women's Court, though, she felt the older woman's arm around her waist, and heard her say quietly, "Shalom."

Joy flooded through her, and she forgot all else. She was coming into the house of the Lord, as she had dreamed of it back in Galilee.

Then she gasped as she glimpsed the great Nicanor Gate of bronze that gleamed like gold. "That was given by a man from Alexandria," said Joab's mother. "It is so heavy that they say it takes twenty men to open it." Deborah gazed in awe at this mighty gate.

"Only men can go into the next court," Joab's mother explained, "but we can go up on one of the galleries and look over the wall." Deborah nodded, breathless, still gazing at the shining gate.

Gently, Joab's mother took her arm and they climbed the steps, listening to the chanting that rose above the other noises of the temple. There was the fragrance of incense and more dazzling white marble as they looked over the wall. There in the center was the huge, rough altar of sacrifice.

"Why is it not carved of marble, too?" Deborah whispered. She need not have whispered, people were walking and talking throughout the Women's Court.

Joab's mother answered quietly, "The altar is of stone, rough stone just as God created it, not hewn by tools of man."

Slowly Deborah nodded. Finally she turned back to look at the Women's Court in more detail. It was still crowded, but from the raised gallery she could see beautiful, trumpet-shaped chests along the walls. Thirteen of them, she counted. How she wished her own mother could have been with her to explain, but before she had time to ask, Joab's mother was speaking again. "Now I must go to the farthest one of the trumpets. That's the one for offerings to maintain the temple."

She started down the steps, and Deborah hurried after her. As they got to the main floor, she felt the older woman slip a coin into her hand. "Give this," she said, "for your sister and the babe. Just walk around and look at the signs on the trumpet chests, then decide where you would like to give."

Deborah hesitated, but she realized this coin was given in kindness. She smiled and nodded and walked slowly away, moving from one trumpet to the next. With a little prayer for Sarah, Deborah dropped her coin into the chest labeled "Sacrifice After Childbirth."

Farther away, Joab's mother was completing her own offering. Now and then she stopped to talk with friends, but Deborah was too much interested in all the trumpets to notice the curious glances in her direction.

Eventually they met at the gate where they had come in. From there they worked their way out of the Women's Court and were plunged once more into the scurry and bustle of the daily temple business.

Outside, the servants with the litter were waiting for them, and Deborah stepped thankfully in behind the older woman and sat down. There at their feet was a basket of fruit and damp cloths to wipe their hands.

Joab's mother looked at Deborah and smiled. "Tired, little one?" As Deborah nodded, the other woman leaned back against the cushions. "Wealth has its advantages, sometimes, does it not?"

Deborah nodded ruefully. "I would rather have stood all day with the sheep than try to push my way through the streets to go home."

Then she gestured toward her skirt. "My lovely robe is soiled, too, where someone stepped—" She stopped abruptly as she stared at the hem. Not only was there the outline of the sandal, but the whole edge of her skirt was dusty where it had brushed along the cobblestones.

Joab's mother reached over and patted her hand. "Don't worry. Joab can't say you didn't wear it." She smiled mischievously. "He wasn't sure, you know. But it doesn't show much down there. Look at mine." She pulled at her skirt to show that it too was dusty along the bottom. "And anyway, silk will wash."

"It will?" gasped Deborah. "Oh, thank goodness. I didn't know. I thought I had ruined it."

Her companion nodded. "That's what I thought when my husband first brought me silk." She was silent, remembering. Then she went on softly. "It was wine color. He has always liked me to wear that color." Then she said more briskly, "Wash it gently and hang it in the shade to dry. You'll see. Besides, Joab will be pleased to buy you another. One is never enough of anything for him."

"Oh, no," protested Deborah. "He must not. It is not fitting. Please tell him."

"Joab is a man, my dear. He is my son, but not a little boy for me to tell him what to do. He makes up his own mind."

"But not mine," Deborah answered rebelliously. "Surely he must realize—I only accepted this because—" she bit her lip. She must not be so rude as to contradict Joab's mother.

But the latter only smiled as she picked an orange from the basket. "It's hard to remember sometimes," she said gently, "that a husband always makes the decisions. But you will learn, and in return, he will give you the best of everything."

The rest of the trip back to Bethany was very quiet. Joab's mother nodded off to sleep, and Deborah stared ahead unseeing as she tried to sort out her thoughts and feelings.

When she got home, she was almost too tired to

talk, but everyone wanted to hear all about the day. They sat in the cool of the courtyard, Elon leaning against Aunt Anna until he fell asleep, and Lamech sitting by Sarah as she nursed the baby.

First Deborah told about the camels and sheep and donkeys, knowing Elon would like to hear about them. After he fell asleep, she told the others about the crowds of people, the brilliance of the temple, the incense and chanting.

"And how did you get along with Joab's mother?" asked Sarah.

"She was very kind to me."

"Yes, but did you like her? Do you feel better about marrying into his family?"

"Sarah!" her husband protested.

But Deborah answered quietly, "I liked her very much." Then to tease her sister a little, she laughed and added as she stood up, "But I would not be marrying her!"

Still, Sarah had the last word. "If you live in their house, you'll be with her more than you will with Joab."

Deborah stood quietly thinking about that, then without answering, went into the house.

11

Early the next day Deborah borrowed a needle from Sarah and very carefully drew the pulled threads in her sleeve back into place. Then she washed the robe carefully and hung it in the shade as Joab's mother had advised her.

When she had finished with that, she went to the village well again and again to fill the big water jar. She washed for Sarah and the baby, for Elon and Aunt Anna. It was a satisfaction to scrub things and see them come clean. Keeping busy helped her not to think too much about the day before. Twice during the day she moved the turquoise gown to be sure it stayed in the shade. To her relief there were no stains where it had been soiled, and it shimmered as beautifully as before.

The next few days were spent quietly. Much as she tried to be helpful, there was really little for Deborah to do. Sarah was busy with the baby, of course, and Aunt Anna loved to bustle around getting meals. Deborah enjoyed little Elon, but even watching him left her much time to think.

She was beginning to get uneasy about things to be done at home and about her father himself. Had his leg entirely healed? Besides, he would be happier in his own home, kind as the neighbors might be. Neighbors—that made her think of Onan—and Judith, of course, she added quickly to herself. She had been away nearly a month already. Surely she would be happy to stay for the sacrifice at the temple following the birth of Sarah's child. That was always on the fortieth day after a little boy was born. And she really wanted to see the temple again, but maybe after that . . .

One evening as they were all sitting in the courtyard, a messenger from Joab's house appeared at the gate. He bowed and spoke directly to Lamech. "My master invites you and your family to supper in his house tomorrow evening. His mother said she especially hoped your wife and new son would be able to come."

Lamech glanced at Sarah and could see her eyes shining at the thought of the invitation. With dignity he stood and answered. "We are most honored. Please tell your master and his mother we will be glad to join them in their home tomorrow evening."

The servant bowed and left. Sarah could hardly wait till he turned the corner before she began to exclaim, to plan what she could wear, and to ask Aunt Anna's advice on how she should dress the children.

Deborah sat silent, trembling. What did Joab's family think? Entertaining her whole family made it almost—yet what could she have done? Lamech was the one to decide whether they should go. Of course, he was thinking of Sarah. Deborah wished she were home. She wished she had never come. No, not that. She cuddled sleepy little Elon closer to her.

"You will wear the turquoise robe, won't you?" Sarah was saying.

Thinking of Sarah's linen ones, Deborah started to answer, "I don't think—"

"Oh, you must," Sarah interrupted. "It's so beautiful, and besides Joab will want you to."

Deborah knew that was true, so she finally agreed.

The next day was rushed as they prepared for the evening. There were all the usual things to do, as well as clothes to be washed and made ready for the visit. Besides, Sarah had to run to her neighbors and tell them of the invitation, with hints at what it might mean for their family. Lamech was home before sundown so that he, too, could wash and put on a fresh robe.

When they arrived at Joab's home, they were welcomed with cool water to wash their hands and feet, and wine to start the evening. Deborah had dreaded coming, but Joab spoke to her so casually it was as if they were old friends, except that she saw his eyes light up when he noticed her gown.

When he introduced her to his father, she hardly dared look up, but one glance showed how much his son looked like him. There was a twinkle in his eye, though, and she couldn't help smiling back. Joab's mother greeted her cordially but could not rest till she was holding the baby. "Oh, when shall I have a grandson like you?" she murmured. Deborah felt herself blush, but everyone else was talking so busily she didn't think they had heard.

They soon gathered about the table. The women were to eat with the men. Deborah was not used to that when there were guests. Still, she was relieved that there were benches for them to sit on instead of the couches she had heard some wealthy people used. The food was delicious. After a little, a servant came in and played his harp softly in the background. Deborah could see Aunt Anna and Joab's mother were having a good visit, and the men were talking business so steadily they paid no attention to her and Sarah.

The two girls were soon chattering away as if they were at home, except that Deborah could see Sarah's eyes noticing the hangings and the candlesticks and the dishes. Thinking how her sister would describe the beautiful things tomorrow, she smiled to herself. Then as she looked up, she realized that Joab was looking at her, even though he was talking to Lamech. She thought, *This is what it would be like to be in his family.* Hesitantly, she smiled at him, then lowered her eyes so no one else would notice.

Before she realized how late it was, Lamech was saying they must be on their way home. "The children will be tired tomorrow," he explained. "And my wife," he added with a smile, though Sarah protested.

As they were leaving, Joab's mother kissed Deborah on both cheeks, and his father, looking at her keenly, said quietly, "You will be welcome in our home at any time."

Deborah thanked him formally for his kindness, but she was breathless when Joab added his farewell. "Have you been happy tonight, little one?" he asked. She nodded, but could find no words to say. Gently he touched her hand as she turned to join the rest of the family.

For days afterward, as Deborah had expected, Sarah could talk of nothing but that evening. She wondered what seasoning had been used on the roasted lamb, and whether there might have been a touch of mint in the bread. The dining room had been almost as cool as a courtyard, with the windows set so they caught every little breeze. And the mosaic floor: Had Deborah noticed the colors of the tiles? It must have been terribly expensive to have had that laid. Wouldn't it be wonderful to have servants enough so you didn't have to scrub the floor for yourself? And the dishes—did Deborah suppose they had come from Greece, with that design in them?

Deborah had noticed many things. It was a beautiful home. As Sarah chattered on, she nodded and agreed, but was really thinking of the people. She remembered Joab's smile. It made her feel so special. He had been nice to her family, too. And his father. He had not been so . . . so . . . Deborah could not think of just the word, but she had thought he would be very proud. She had expected to be embarrassed in such a rich house, but really he just seemed to take things for granted.

She sighed. Would she be able to make Joab proud of her, as his mother had learned to do when she married? Would she ever learn how to manage servants and make an elegant home?

Sarah got up and started to make fresh bread for supper. Deborah smiled to herself. Too bad Sarah had not been married to Joab. She would have delighted in a house like that. Well, that wasn't the way things worked. But when she and Joab were married—

Deborah was startled out of her dreaming. She had thought *when* not *if* she and Joab were married. Did that mean her mind was made up? Her hands had suddenly become quiet, and she was staring at them without seeing, when Lamech came in from work.

Hastily she put down her yarn and went to help Sarah wash up the vegetables and pour fresh water for supper. Lamech washed his hands and feet, then played a few minutes with Elon before he sat down to eat.

The days were going by swiftly. At last it was time for the whole family to go to the temple. It didn't seem possible to Deborah she had been here more than forty days.

When that morning dawned, everybody was up early, for it was a very special day. Lamech had hired a donkey for Sarah to ride on and another for Aunt Anna. Deborah had insisted she wanted to walk this time.

"But your lovely robe—" Sarah had started to protest.

"I shall wear my linen one," Deborah had answered firmly. "I am part of this family—and not the most important part either," she added, giving Sarah a quick hug. "I shall dress as you do and walk with Elon, at least till he gets tired. He will want to pick flowers or perhaps catch grasshoppers along the way. How could I do that dressed in silk?"

In the end she had her way, and they set out on the road to Jerusalem just after sunrise. They had packed bread and fruit for their lunch after the sacrifice, and Aunt Anna had that bundle tied to her saddle. Sarah, of course, was carrying the baby. It was still cool, and as they walked along the ancient road, Deborah could almost imagine herself back on the caravan route in Galilee.

She talked to Elon about his grandfather and about Onan who would be leading their flocks out already. When he was bigger and could come to visit, he could climb the old olive trees, or even an oak. She told him about her friend Judith and her little Azi, who was younger than Elon but bigger than the new baby. She helped him climb up on a stone wall and walk carefully along the top, standing taller than any of them. When he got to the end of the wall, he jumped down and picked a handful of poppies for his mother.

By that time his legs were getting tired, so Aunt Anna took him up to ride ahead of her. As Lamech was walking with Sarah, Deborah was left to her own thoughts.

Naturally they turned to Joab. He had really been nice to her and her family. And his mother and father had made her feel so welcome. That was important if she was to live there with them. His mother surely would help her learn how to manage the household. But what about Joab himself? Would he be more like his mother when she got to know him better? Or would she always have to be careful what she said? He had said she must be proud. But would he be proud of her? Or just be proud of what he bought for her? That wasn't nice.

She shut the thought out of her mind, but then she remembered the two haughty ladies in the temple. Was that what he wanted? Surely not, or he would not have chosen her in the first place. He did choose her. She smiled to herself. He really cared about her. Besides, her father said he was a good man. It would be all right.

12

WHEN THE GOLDEN RIM of the temple came into view, Deborah's heart lifted. Surely the Lord was here. How else could men have dreamed of this building and planned it and built it? No wonder Jewish people who lived in other countries came here whenever they could to offer sacrifices to the living God!

This day she did not mind the crowds and the cries, the bustle and the pushing. Not having to worry about her rich robe, she felt more a part of the crowd. She could imagine her father bringing the lambs to market, and she could look into the shops for copper and leather and pottery. She wondered if Joab had gotten the pottery sheep here.

Slowly they climbed up the grand stairs to the temple. This must be the better way to approach the Lord, walking with His people, as plain as the mighty rock of His altar.

When they entered the Court of the Gentiles, Lamech left them standing by a pillar and went to change money and arrange the purchase of the two turtledoves for sacrifice. When he came back, he led the family into the Court of the Women. Here Deborah took charge of Elon. She and Aunt Anna sat on a bench by the wall where they would be out of the way but could still see the great Nicanor Gate. While Sarah held the baby, Lamech dropped the coins for the sacrifice into the third trumpet. Then he and Sarah climbed the steps to the great shining gate. There Sarah stood on the gallery with other new mothers, where they could look over the wall, but Lamech went through the gate to the inner court. Almost immediately the deep sound of music announced that the ceremony was starting.

Elon stared around at the crowds of people, but finally he crept closer to Deborah. "I want my father," he said softly.

"I know," she answered. "He will be back in just a few minutes."

Actually it was more than a few minutes, but Elon was reassured and waited quietly. At last Lamech emerged, and with Sarah and the baby he came to where the others were waiting. "Now we shall celebrate," he said, taking Elon's hand.

As they left the temple, he stopped to buy honey cakes in a little shop, and a small skin of wine to mix with the water they had brought.

"Can I have a cake right now?" Elon asked.

His father smiled. "Just a bite in honor of your mother and your little brother," he said.

"Two bites," bargained Elon, but his father only laughed and shook his head. "One bite now, another after lunch," he promised.

Elon was satisfied with the piece his father broke off for him, and soon they found a place to stop for lunch. It was in the shade of the city wall, but out of the way of the passersby. Lamech tethered the donkeys while the family found rocks to sit on and opened the food bundles. Soon they were all peeling oranges and breaking bread from the big, flat loaves Sarah had baked yesterday.

Before the lunch was finished, Elon had fallen asleep against his father. The others sat visiting quietly, talking about the temple and the people they had seen, and waiting for the heat of the day to pass.

When they finally started down the street that would take them back to Bethany, a friend of Lamech's fell into step with him. "You really ought to hear Him," he was saying as Deborah paused to look into a leather shop. She wished she had brought some coins. She could have gotten new sandals for her father. When she hurried along to catch up with the others, the man had gone on, and Lamech had swung tired little Elon up on his shoulders.

It was nearly dark before they reached home. After a quick supper, everyone was soon in bed. The next morning, though, before he left for work, Lamech told them what his friend had been talking about.

"It seems there's a new rabbi," He said. "In fact," he went on, turning to Deborah, "he comes from up in Galilee near where you live. Have you heard of him? A carpenter named Jesus?"

Deborah shook her head. "Perhaps my father might have, but I've never heard him say."

"Anyway, He comes from Nazareth—"

"Nazareth!" she exclaimed. "I never heard of any special rabbi there."

"They say this man is really special. He heals people just by a word without even touching them. He has friends here in Bethany, so we may see Him sometime."

"Who are the friends?" asked Sarah. "Do we know them?"

"Enoch didn't know. He just said he'd heard the teacher might come to Bethany. I'll ask more about it today to see if anybody in the market knows."

That night Lamech was late coming from work. "Everybody is talking about the new rabbi," he said. "They say this Jesus of Nazareth is coming here some-time soon. He stays at the home of Lazarus when he comes, but wherever people get together, He will stop and talk with them."

"Does He then go back to Nazareth?" Deborah asked. "Do you suppose he would take a message to my father?"

Lamech smiled. "I doubt once He has come to

Jerusalem that he will go back to Nazareth." Then he sobered. "But what message do you want to send? Are you not happy here?"

"Oh, yes. You have been most kind. It has been good to be with Sarah again, and to see the children. But Father should know he has a new grandson."

"You are right. We should have sent the good news. We must see to it when Korah goes north again."

"If he goes soon, perhaps I could go with him instead of just sending a message."

"Oh, not yet," objected Sarah.

"But Father will be needing me. Aunt Anna, you can stay longer to help Sarah, can't you? But Father is alone. Even though Onan's family is good to him, he will want to be back in his own home."

"Yes, I suppose so," Sarah agreed slowly. "But you should not be traveling alone."

"Korah is kinsman. Surely I would be safe in his caravan."

The next day Lamech brought the news that Korah would be going to Nazareth again in about five days. Deborah would be welcome in the caravan if she cared to go, but they were going the longer way, across the Jordan, to avoid bandits this time in Samaria.

"Can I go, too?" asked Elon.

"Oh, Elon," said his mother. "It's a long trip. Besides, what would I do without you?"

"You've got the new baby," Elon answered. "I want to go with Aunt Deborah."

"Oh, do let him, Sarah," urged Deborah. "He would be company for me, and he should see his grandfather."

Lamech scooped Elon up in his arms. "It's a long ways, you know. Could you be a big boy and not cry when your legs got tired?"

Elon nodded. "I don't cry anymore—not much, anyway. And I could rest when the donkeys do."

His father laughed. "Another little donkey," he teased, but he and Sarah were looking at each other.

"When could we bring him back?" she asked.

"Can't he stay all summer?" asked Deborah. "He could go out with Father when he leads the sheep, and he could play with Azi. And there's plenty of room for him to run and climb trees—" she broke off, thinking of the last time she had climbed a tree, but nobody noticed.

"Please, please," begged Elon. "I want to see all the sheep."

Lamech set him carefully on the ground. "I don't see why he shouldn't," he said thoughtfully. "I was going to hire a donkey for Deborah, anyway. He could ride with her. Then later when I take Aunt Anna home, I could bring him back."

"That would be perfect," agreed Deborah. Then she squatted down to talk to Elon. "Do you want to ride on a donkey with me?"

He flung his arms around her neck. "Ride on a donkey and see Grandfather's sheep!" Then he went racing around the courtyard. "I'm going to ride on a donkey and see lots of sheep," he chanted, as the others looked at him and each other and laughed.

Every day when he woke up, Elon asked if it was time to go, but it was four days before Korah was ready to set out. Sarah had packed Elon clean clothes in a bundle. In another she had packed bread and figs and dates for Elon to lunch on between their regular meals.

When Deborah began to pack her own clothes, she hesitated over the silk robe. She would never wear it in Galilee, but she could not give it back, and Sarah could not wear it. If she were married to Joab of course . . . She was more comfortable about him now that she had met his family, but still . . .

"Father will just have to decide," she murmured, and packed the robe with her other clothes. She wondered whether she should send word that she was leaving, but somehow that seemed to take too much for granted, as if she were betrothed and her comings and goings were important to his family.

The morning that they left, Elon was so excited he could not eat any breakfast, and Deborah was almost as bad. It seemed so long since she had seen her father, and Judith and Onan, of course. There was a flurry of good-byes and thank-yous and cries of "May the Lord keep you safe." Before sunrise they joined the caravan with Elon riding in front of Deborah and the bundles fastened on behind.

After they passed Jericho, they came at last to the Jordan River and camped near it that night. Elon had never seen so much water before. Deborah let him wade in the shallow edge before they had supper.

It was a long journey for little Elon. At first it was exciting to be riding the donkey and seeing everything new. When he got too tired, he went to sleep held tight in Deborah's arms. Sometimes they got down from the donkey and walked. They looked for pretty stones and for flowers and for little lizards as they went along.

Before the end of the third day, though, Elon was asking how much farther it was, and Deborah was remembering all the stories she could think of to tell him. She told him of David and Goliath, and Daniel in the lions' den, and the manna that God had sent down to feed His people in the wilderness.

One afternoon they stopped a little early, for they had come to a good open place with a brook for water. Besides, the leader of a caravan coming south had told Korah that the new rabbi people were talking about was coming this way. Like everyone else, Deborah wanted to hear Him.

She could see people who must have followed them from Jericho or Jerusalem, and other people were gathering from the countryside. One time she even thought she saw Joab, but it was just a glimpse, and she decided she must have been mistaken. Of course, he could have heard of this new rabbi and come to hear Him on his way to some other business. With the crowd growing, she kept Elon by her and made sure their donkey was tethered close to Korah's.

13

IT WAS ALMOST SUNDOWN when a shout went up, "He comes! He comes!" People began gathering in a circle about the rabbi and his friends. Out of respect they left a space clear around the big rock where He could sit and be heard.

He talked plainly to them about the responsibilities of marriage. Deborah saw Korah getting nearer and nearer to the teacher, so she took Elon by the hand and led him quietly along to stay near her kinsman. Suddenly one of the rabbi's friends stopped her. "Take the child to the back. He is not old enough to understand."

Deborah bowed her head in embarrassment and turned back, but then she heard the rabbi say, "Let the little children come to Me, and do not hinder them, for the kingdom of God belongs to such as these." As she looked up, she saw Him hold out His arms while He was still speaking. Confidently Elon let go of her hand and walked up to the rabbi, who put one hand on the little boy's head and blessed him. At once other women started pushing their children nearer.

Deborah edged forward and picked up Elon. She carried him away, and they sat down near Korah till the crowd stilled again. Then she saw the rabbi stand as if He were about to leave, but a young man ran up to Him and knelt.

Deborah gasped. Joab! It was he! But why was he kneeling to a strange rabbi? Then she realized he was speaking. ". . . what must I do to inherit eternal life?"

Tensely she listened and heard the rabbi repeating the commandments Moses had given them from God.

Then she heard Joab answer, "Master, all these I have kept since I was a boy."

Deborah let out her breath quietly. That was true, she was sure. Her father had said he was a good man.

But the teacher was speaking again. "You still lack one thing. Sell everything you have and give to the poor, and you will have treasure in heaven. . . ."

Slowly Joab stood. He looked as if he were going to argue, but instead he bowed his head and turned away. He looked like a little boy who had been scolded.

Deborah's heart went out to him. She wanted to comfort him as she would Elon.

She stood up and whispered, "Come," to Elon. "That is the man who gave you the nice, big sheep. We will go and speak to him."

Elon hung back, but she pulled on his hand and hurried toward the edge of the crowd. Joab was standing with his back to them. The crowd was moving now, and the rabbi was walking away with his followers.

"Joab," she said quietly.

He swung around and stared at her. The blood rushed to his face, and he looked so angry Deborah could not remember what she had intended to say. "What are you doing here?" he demanded. "Spying on me? Pushing yourself in with all these men?"

"I didn't—" she started, but he cut her off.

"I don't know who He thinks He is to tell me to throw away all my property. My father worked hard to get it, and anyway, how can I honor my father and mother, as the commandment says, if I don't have money to do it with?"

Deborah could see he had been disappointed at the answer and was more angry at the rabbi than at her. Softly she said, "There are other ways—" But he would not listen.

"I follow the commandments and I give alms to the poor. I do all that the law requires." Suddenly he saw the compassion in Deborah's face. "Don't look at me like that. You don't need to be sorry for me. I own more sheep than your father will ever have, and land to pasture them."

"But do you know your sheep?" she asked gently.

"Of course not. Why should I? I have servants to do that."

Deborah could feel Elon pulling at her hand. Swiftly she picked him up and hushed him.

Just then Joab realized that some of the men around were watching. "Come," he said sharply. "Gather your bundles. I will take you back to Lamech's house."

She shook her head. "I am going to my father's house," she explained. "I am with a kinsman."

Now Joab was really angry with her. "You will do as I say!"

But she was stiffly angry, too. "I will do as my father says," she replied.

He gave a bitter laugh. "We shall see. Tomorrow I will send one more offer to your father, and it will be one he cannot refuse. I can pay for whatever I want. Then when you are in my house, you will obey me!"

He turned and left her standing there. Elon put his arms around her neck. "Bad man," he said.

Deborah cuddled his head against her shoulder. "No," she said, "he means to be good. We will go back to Korah now and sleep by our donkey. Soon we will get to our house, and you will see Grandfather's sheep."

"And Onan's?" asked Elon.

At once Deborah felt a surge of relief. "Yes, we will see Onan's sheep, too," she agreed. "Sleep quickly, for tomorrow will come soon."

Elon did go to sleep quickly, and so did Deborah, though she had not expected to.

It was to be two more days before they would cross

the Jordan again and begin to see the hills of Galilee. They followed the valley for miles. In places the river spread out in wide, shallow curves, then the banks narrowed, and the water came bubbling and boiling through the narrow channels and down stony rapids.

"When will we get there?" Elon kept asking. "How much longer before we get to Grandfather's house?"

He and Deborah were both too excited to ride for long at a time. Often they slid off and led the donkey along the narrow path.

The last morning Deborah remembered a game she used to play with Judith and Onan. She and Elon looked for twelve tiny stones, one for each tribe of Israel. That took some time, especially as Deborah tried to teach him all the tribes: Levi and Benjamin and Reuben and Simeon and all the others. When she had all twelve pebbles in her hand, she called, "Get ready!" Elon held out his hands with their backs up. She tossed the tiny stones gently into the air and turned her hand with its back up, too. Whoever caught more of the pebbles on his hand won the game.

"I got only two," complained Elon.

"Then you won," answered Deborah. "I caught just one. Hurry now. We must not lag behind. We'll play again, maybe when the donkeys stop at noon. Next time you can throw the stones."

"We'll have to get more stones, though," Elon pointed out.

"That's right," Deborah agreed. "The tribes always

get scattered, but we'll get them together again. How many names can you remember?"

By afternoon Elon was willing to get back on the donkey and snuggle down against Deborah for his nap. Deborah was glad to have him quiet as they got nearer and nearer to Nazareth. She wondered if Joab had sent a messenger to her father by the shorter way through Samaria. If he had, she wondered what his message had been. And what her father had replied.

She turned her mind away from that and wondered how Judith's Azi had grown. And Onan—she suddenly cuddled Elon extra tight in her arms. She remembered how Onan had looked when she left. "Come back safe," he had said. That was all, but somehow she felt safe just thinking about him.

At last they came in sight of Nazareth, nestled in its own little part of the valley. "Wake up, Elon," she cried. "Wake up. We're almost there."

He sat up and looked around. "Where?" he asked.

Deborah laughed happily. "There," she said, pointing ahead. "That's Nazareth, and farther up are your grandfather's sheep. Are you really awake? Can you carry one of the bundles? Oh, no, you have your little sheep. I'll tell Korah we're going to walk from here. You stay by the donkey, and I'll be right back."

Deborah darted toward the head of the caravan and was back in just a few minutes. Hastily she untied one of the bundles. "There, we'll leave the others, and I'll get them later. We'll go across the fields now."

"Will Onan's sheep be there, too?" Elon asked.

"Somewhere near," she answered. "He has to take them where the feed is good, so he may be farther away. But we'll see him by night anyway."

They started scrambling up the hills. Oh, it was good to be home! "Look, Elon, there's a hawk up in the sky. How would you like to fly like that?"

"Would he take me on his back?" he asked.

"I'm afraid not." Deborah laughed as she glanced down at him. "You're pretty big for a hawk to carry. But you can jump off a rock and pretend you're flying. Judith and I used to do that, but we didn't dare jump off as high rocks as Onan did. He would wave his arms and pretend he was an eagle."

"There are lots of trees," said Elon almost fearfully. "Are robbers hiding behind them?"

"Oh, no," said Deborah. "We don't have any robbers here. We're all friends. The trees are for shade when it gets hot at noon. And for climbing," she added. "You can climb up in an oak tree or an olive tree and look all over the valley."

"I never climbed a tree," said Elon.

"I know," answered Deborah, "but I have. We'll pick a good one to climb."

"Will Onan climb a tree with me?" Elon asked.

"Oh, I'm sure," she agreed.

Suddenly Deborah stopped. There on the path ahead stood Onan. He looked at her, and she looked at him, and neither spoke a word.

14

DEBORAH FELT BREATHLESS, but she knew she must say something. "How did you know—" she started.

"I've been watching every day. When I saw the caravan coming, I hoped—I thought it might be you." He was still looking steadily at her. "You know we can see quite a ways down the valley."

She felt herself flushing, and tried to turn his attention. "Especially if you climb a tree! This is Elon, Sarah's son. He wants to know if you will climb a tree with him. Elon, this is Onan."

Elon nodded solemnly. "You made a sheep for me," he said, holding it up.

Onan glanced at it, then shook his head. "I didn't make a woolly one," he said.

Elon explained. "His leg broke, and Aunt Deborah fixed it. But you made the sheep. She said so."

A smile spread over Onan's face. "Did you like your sheep?" he asked Elon, but he was looking at Deborah.

She nodded. "He would not let us leave it behind." Then hurriedly she asked, "How is Father?"

"He's fine," Onan answered. "He will be anxious to see you." He squatted down by Elon. "Climb on my back, and I'll give you a ride. We'll go see the sheep."

It was a joyous reunion as Deborah ran to her father, and he clasped her in his arms. "Are you well?" he asked softly. "And Sarah?"

"Oh, Father, you have a new grandson. Sarah is well and so is the baby. Aunt Anna is going to stay with her a little longer, but I wanted to come home." She turned back to where Onan and Elon were now standing. "Here is Elon, your firstborn grandson," she said. "He's quite grown up since you saw him last. Come, Elon," she called, holding out her hand. "This is your grandfather." Elon held up his face for the kiss of welcome, but he hung onto Deborah's hand.

She went on, "We'll go to the house now. It will soon be time for supper." Turning to Onan she invited, "Will you eat with us?"

He shook his head. "You are tired and will have much to talk about with your father. Perhaps I will see you tomorrow." He bowed formally and turned away.

Deborah looked at him in astonishment. Onan bowing to her? She turned back to her father and surprised a little smile on his face.

He said nothing to her, though, but put his hand on Elon's head. "I'm glad you came, little man," he said warmly, and Elon smiled up at him.

"I'm glad I did, too," he said. "Can I play with the real sheep tomorrow?"

His grandfather shook his head. "The sheep are too busy eating to have time to play," he said, "but you can watch them with me and learn their names."

Elon went off contented, holding Deborah's hand. When her father came in that night from the sheepfold, Deborah had barley bread baking and porridge cooking by the fire, and cucumbers fresh from the garden. She bustled around to set cups of fresh water by each place and wash Elon's hands and face.

At first she asked about the neighbors and about the sheep and about people Judith had just had time to mention before they each started supper. When they sat down to eat, though, she was quiet. There seemed so much to tell her father, but so little she wanted to say in front of Elon. Still, he was so tired he almost went to sleep before he finished his porridge.

"It's been a long day," his grandfather said with a smile, and Deborah nodded.

"I'm not tired," said Elon, but he made no protest as Deborah laid out his sleeping pad and settled him on it. He was asleep before she finished washing the supper dishes.

At last she went out and sat by her father in the courtyard. There was a little breeze, and the stars were beginning to come out. They sat silently for several minutes before her father spoke. "It is good to have you home, my daughter."

"It is good to be here," she answered. Then she took a deep breath. "Did Joab send you a—a message?"

"He did, but I have not yet given a reply."

"He said it would be an offer you could not refuse."

Calmly he answered, "I can refuse anything the Lord God would not have me do."

"But how do you know what He would have you do?"

"I think He will have put the answer in your heart. Is that not why you came home?"

"I was—worried—"

"Did you not trust me, then?"

"Oh, yes, but you weren't there. I was confused, and I didn't have anybody to talk with who understood. Sarah thought it would be a fine marriage, and his mother was kind, and sometimes Joab was—exciting—"

"Tell me now. You have been so busy with Elon and our supper—Did you have a happy time?"

"At first, I did," she said. "The trip to Bethany was beautiful, and I could hardly wait to see Sarah, and Joab was so brave when the bandits attacked. Or I thought he was," she added.

She sat remembering, and her father waited. At last it all came tumbling out: the silk dress, Joab's stepping on Elon's toy, the elegant new sheep, the trips to the temple, things Joab's mother had said, the supper at their house, the rabbi's blessing of Elon, his answer to Joab's questions, and Joab's anger. She felt exhausted and yet at peace when she had finished. Now she could see the whole pattern more clearly.

Her father put his hand on her head as he had before. "Then is it not plain what our answer should be?" he asked gently.

"But if Joab would give a bride price big enough to buy more sheep for you—"

"Did you not listen to the rabbi?" her father asked sternly. "Would you have me rich at the cost of my daughter?"

"But he will be angry. He might do damage—"

"No, he is a man who abides by the law. You may feel safe. He will not break the law. It's just that we need more than the law to be happy. And I want you happy."

Deborah's heart lifted. She did feel safe. And yet there was an emptiness. She had thought she would be married. And now she would not.

"Rest quietly tonight," her father said at last. "We will talk again, but tonight you are as tired as Elon." Deborah could hear the smile in his voice as they stood, and comforted, she walked into the house to sleep.

The next morning Elon was up as soon as he heard his grandfather stirring. "Are we going to take care of the sheep now, Grandfather?" he asked.

"As soon as you eat your breakfast," he answered, going out to see what the weather promised.

Deborah smiled happily to herself. It was so good to have everything peaceful and orderly and to be back in her own home. She dressed Elon and settled him with a piece of bread and a cup of goat's milk borrowed from Judith.

When he had finished, he started for the door with his grandfather. "Aren't you coming, too?" he asked, turning back to Deborah.

"No, I'll bring your lunch at noon," she answered. "You go now. Here are some raisins in case you get hungry before I come." She handed him a cluster, and he ran to catch up with his grandfather.

As soon as they were gone, Deborah took all the sleeping pads out to air. With them in the sunshine, she set to work sweeping the hearth and the floor. Next she scrubbed the pots that had not been used while she was away and ground some more grain to fill the bin. She had checked the vat for olives. It was still nearly half full, and there were dried dates in the cupboard. She was just thinking she would make some new bread for their lunch when Judith came to the door.

"Now we'll have time to talk," she called. "Bring your jar and we'll go to the well for water. Oh, Deborah, I can't wait to hear all about your trip." She came on into the room. "Was it exciting? Did you go to the temple?" She lowered her voice. "Did you meet Joab's family?"

Deborah had picked up the water jar, but now she set it down again. "Oh, Judith, what am I going to say? Everybody will want to know everything about them."

Judith stopped smiling. "I did not mean to pry," she said stiffly.

Deborah ran and flung her arms around her. "I didn't mean you. Oh, I've got so many things to tell you. But the older women—they think I should be married already." The tears began to spill down her face. "They'll think I wasn't good enough. They'll say his family sent me back. But it wasn't that way at all."

"Of course it wasn't." Judith shook her. "Now stop crying and we'll think what to say."

Shamefaced, Deborah wiped up her tears. "I'm sorry. I didn't mean to be so foolish. I don't know why—"

"I do," Judith answered softly. "When I'm excited, I'm just as apt to cry as to laugh. My husband says I'm silly, but that's the way it is."

"But what shall I say?" Deborah asked helplessly.

15

Judith laughed. "Don't worry," she said. "Tell everybody what a wonderful time you had. And tell them about Sarah's new baby. Everybody wants to know about a new baby. That's what you went for, isn't it? Just pretend you don't know what they mean if they ask you anything else."

Deborah began to giggle. "And I did go to the temple. Oh, Judith, it is beautiful. I can tell them all about it. And the new rabbi—no, not that—but the crowds of people and the shops in the marketplace. . . ."

She picked up the water jar, and the two girls started for the well chattering so fast they only greeted the women they saw, without stopping to talk.

When they got back, it was time for Deborah to pack lunch for her father and Elon. She put in extra, too, because Onan would probably be there.

When she got to her father's flock, though, Onan

was not there. "Did you learn all the sheep's names?" she asked Elon.

"That's Pepper," he said, pointing to a little black lamb. "And that's Jumper," he added, pointing to another. "He jumped right up in the air like this." He tried to show her, but almost fell over.

Deborah laughed and began laying out the food on the cloth that had covered her basket. Casually she asked, "Did Onan help you climb a tree?"

"No, he didn't come. Grandfather said he's way over there with those sheep."

"Well, maybe he'll come this afternoon."

Her father walked quietly from the flock and sat down.

When they had finished eating, he asked, "Did you bring your spinning?"

Deborah nodded. "I thought I would sit here in the shade while Elon has his nap."

"Will you have a nap, too?" Elon asked his grandfather.

"No, I'll be leading the sheep farther this afternoon. They have nearly finished grazing here. When you wake up, your Aunt Deborah will help you find me."

"All right," agreed Elon. He snuggled down with a date in his hand, but he was asleep before he could bite into it.

Deborah had looked forward to spinning there in the shade, but somehow she could not settle peacefully to it. She would spin for a little while, then stand and look for the sheep. She could see her father easily, but Onan seemed to be leading his flock farther away. She would sit down again, but her fingers were tense, and she tangled the yarn.

At last she gave up and lay down beside Elon. It seemed only a minute before she heard him whisper, "Aunt Deborah, are you asleep?"

She sat up. "I must have been," she said, smiling. "See how far the sun has gone. We must go find Grandfather's sheep."

Before they started out, she took one swift look in the other direction, but Onan's sheep were no longer in sight. For a moment she had a sickening thought. Had he quarreled with her father about something? But she put it aside. Her father would not have been happy if there were trouble between him and a neighbor. It must be just that the grass was getting scarcer for two flocks to be near.

That evening Deborah and her father again sat in the courtyard after Elon had gone to sleep. They were quiet for some time, listening to the locusts. Finally her father started to speak. "You told me of your time in Bethany. Now I will tell you what has happened since you left."

"Oh, Father, is something wrong? I wondered, when Onan did not come."

"No, there is reason for that, but not, I think, an unhappy one. Onan has grown up while you have been away."

"Grown up? But he was grown up. He's eighteen."

"Nineteen, now," said her father with a smile, "but that is not what I meant. He has always been a good boy, but not very serious, perhaps. While you have been gone, I think he has thought what it would be like if you were not to come back. He has thought what he wants his life to be."

Deborah sat, waiting, until her father went on. "Onan asked his father to talk with me, and he did. He came especially, seven days ago. He would be happy to have you for a daughter-in-law. He has increased the flock Onan will have when he is married, though he realizes that is still small compared with what you would have in the house of Joab. Therefore, he asked me to say nothing till we knew whether you wanted to stay in Bethany. That way Onan would not be shamed in the village, for such things get talked about."

Deborah's heart began pounding. "But what about Joab?" she whispered. "Have you sent word to him?"

"I sent a message this morning. I said I was honored by his kindnesses and would always hold him and his family in great respect. But I felt my daughter was not prepared to take such a position as he offered. Also, as my wife was no longer living, I would prefer to have my daughter near me."

Deborah grasped her father's hand and held it to her cheek. He put out his other hand and brushed back a lock of her hair. "You are not hurt that I said you were unprepared for such a position? I know you could fulfill it well, if that is what you desired, but the first and the last of what I said are true, at least."

She shook her head. "That was true, too. I have not been trained to wear a silk robe and to ride in a litter."

The next morning Deborah was up even before her father. Without a sound she took the water jar and headed for the well. Nobody else would be drawing water so early, and she was too excited to lie still any longer. Surely today Onan would come.

After breakfast, her father took little Elon by the hand and they left for the sheepfold. "I will bring lunch at noon," Deborah promised. To Elon she said, "Maybe Onan will help you climb a tree today."

He took a little skip as he agreed, "Climb a tree."

Again that day Deborah packed extra and went swinging her basket up toward the pasture. She knew she was early, but she had left everything in order at the house. She must not burden her father with looking after Elon, she told herself, when he had all the sheep to care for. After all, she was the one who had asked Elon to come.

But when she reached her father's flock, Onan and his flock were way in the distance. Her father said nothing, but Elon pointed. "Grandfather says Onan won't come for lunch. He won't be here to help me climb a tree. I want to climb a tree."

"Then let's go where Onan is," said Deborah decisively. "We'll leave the lunch basket here with Grandfather and go find Onan."

"And climb a tree?" Elon asked hopefully.

"And climb a tree," she echoed.

They set off across the field, Deborah trying to slow her pace to Elon's short steps. He wanted to climb on all the rocks, but she kept hurrying him on. The nearer they got, though, the less sure she was that she had done the right thing. She began slowing down even more than Elon.

Then she saw Onan leave his flock and come toward her. Her heart began to pound. What would he say? Would he think she was bold in coming to him?

She need not have worried. His eyes were on her face as he leaped across a small wadi and ran up the hill. One glance at him was enough to show her the joy in his eyes, but she lowered hers quickly. Breathlessly she said, "Elon thought you would help him climb a tree."

Onan laughed happily. "The way I used to help you?" he teased. Turning to Elon, he suggested, "There's an oak tree with a good low branch to start on over here. Come try it."

When they got to the tree, Onan warned, "Just the first branch today. You have to learn to balance on that before you go up higher." Easily he helped Elon climb onto the lowest limb. "There. You're almost as high as I am. Now reach up. Take hold of the next branch and stand up on this one."

Carefully Elon reached up to the next branch. "I'm not going to fall," he said.

"Of course not," Onan agreed.

Elon stood up on the first branch and looked around. "I can see a long ways," he said.

"That's right," agreed Onan again, "and pretty soon you can climb onto a higher branch and see farther."

"Now?" asked Elon.

"No, you have to learn how to sit down again on the first branch and then jump off by yourself."

"Try it now," encouraged Deborah, "and then we'll go have lunch with Grandfather."

Onan helped Elon keep his balance as he sat down and held one hand as the little boy jumped to the ground.

"Will you come eat with us?" Deborah asked, not looking at him.

Onan shook his head. "It would be too far from my sheep. I will come talk with your father and you this evening."

Deborah nodded and gave one quick glance up before she turned away with Elon. She was sure Onan stood watching as they walked away, but she did not look back.

16

IT WAS WELL AFTER DARK that evening and the moon was high over the hills before Onan came. Elon had long gone to sleep. Deborah and her father as usual were sitting in the courtyard.

Neither was saying anything, but each knew why they were waiting. Deborah's mind drifted back to the evening in Bethany when Joab had come in anger to see her. Now she was at peace instead of listening tensely.

When they heard his sandals, Deborah ran to open the gate. Courteously he greeted her and her father, but shook his head and remained standing when she gestured toward the bench. Formally he turned to her father.

"My father has told me you and he have agreed that your daughter may become my wife." Deborah drew a quick breath as she heard the words. He went on. "I come to tell you that I am happy it is to be so. I will do my best to make her life such as you would want for your daughter."

Her father nodded his head soberly. "I have confidence that you will. Is it your wish then, to be betrothed to my daughter?"

"It is," Onan answered.

Her father turned then to Deborah. "And is it your wish to be betrothed to this man?"

"It is," she whispered.

"Then may the Lord bless this union," said her father solemnly. Then his voice lightened. "Deborah, bring us wine. This is an occasion to be remembered, and we have plans to talk about."

As she came back out of the house, she heard Onan saying, "I am sorry I do not yet have a house of my own for my wife to come to. As my flock grows, I will have one that she may be happy with and that will have room so that you can live with us. In the meantime, my mother welcomes Deborah to our home. Also, you know we live near enough so that she can come to you often to keep your house as she has done."

They were silent as Deborah poured the wine and each one tasted it.

Then her father answered. "You and your family have been most kind to me, and I appreciate your thoughtfulness. However, I would wish my daughter to have her own home."

"I would wish it, too," responded Onan quickly. "Just as soon as I can—"

"I know. But I have thought of another plan. Please do not reject it till you have thought about it. Your father has planned to increase your flock as a marriage gift. I would like, accordingly, to give you this house. It would be Deborah's anyway, when I am through with it. There would be only one stipulation: that I be welcome to live here the rest of my life as you would have lived in your father's house."

"Father!" Deborah exclaimed.

"Welcome!" Onan said in the same moment. "Welcome in your own house!"

"It would not be my house," her father answered calmly. "I would be living with my daughter and her husband, if you would agree." He paused, looking at the two of them, then went on with a smile, "Think about it. Deborah is used to managing her own house, and I would try not to be a difficult father-in-law!"

Onan knelt and seized his hands. "I don't have to think about it, if you really mean it. You've been like a second father to me anyway. It would mean—"

Deborah's father stood and drew Onan up, too. "It would mean you could get married soon, and I would not lose my daughter when you do. Sometime soon our families will meet for the formal betrothal. In the meantime—" He leaned forward and kissed Onan first on one cheek and then on the other. He turned and did the same with Deborah, and went into the house.

After he had gone in, Deborah and Onan sat for some time on the bench under the acacia tree. The moon rose higher as they talked and were silent.

At last Onan said, "It is time I went home, but I have something for you first." He hesitated. "It is not costly."

He stood up, then sat down again, reached out to take her hand and piled it full of beads, closely strung on a fine leather cord. Slowly Deborah raised her hand to let the strand hang from her fingers. The moonlight fell on the beads of delicately carved olive wood, with streaks of light and dark in each bead.

"Onan! They are beautiful," she whispered.

"Each one is different," he said. "I carved them for you from a branch of the tree we used to climb. Will you wear them?"

"With all my heart," she answered. "Will you put them on for me?"

He took the strand from her and stood slipping the beads around in his fingers. Finally he said. "You will have a gold ring for our wedding. Two years ago my grandmother gave me her family ring and said it was for my wife. But I wanted to do something for you myself."

Deborah stepped nearer, and he slipped the beads over her head. As they dropped into place, she reached up and took his hands. They stood together silently for a long moment, then turned and walked toward the gate.

Onan went out and pulled it closed between them. His hands still on the top rail, he said softly, "You know, betrothal is almost marriage. There is no turning back. You are now my wife."

Deborah nodded, secure and happy. Quietly she answered, "And you are—" But she could not finish. She bowed her head as she felt herself flushing.

Gently Onan put his hand under her chin and lifted her face. "Say it," he said.

She looked at him steadily. Then proudly she whispered, "My husband."

ELIZABETH
of Capernaum

Elizabeth had never thought of love until she met Nathan, the handsome young caravan leader. It was a brief meeting . . . she never expected to see him again. And then, there he was one day in the marketplace!

And Nathan cares for Elizabeth, just as she cares for him. Yet, how can they be married? His marriage offer to another girl is binding . . . unless she tires of waiting for Nathan. Elizabeth knows *she* could wait forever.

While she waits, she serves as a companion to Susan, a wise woman of great faith. Who would have known how a meeting with Jesus, the rabbi who performed many miracles, would change both their lives.

Edith E. Cutting's short stories and poems have appeared in many magazines. A retired English teacher, she makes her home in Johnson City, New York.

DAVID C. COOK
PUBLISHING CO.